Heart of Glass
A Killer Love Story

CRAIG WALLWORK

Copyright @ 2020 by Craig Wallwork.
All rights reserved, including the rights to reproduce this book or portions thereof in any form whatsoever.

ISBN: 9798694034272

This is a work of fiction. Names, characters, places and incidents either are the product of the author's imagination or are used fictitiously. Any resemblance to actual persons, living or dead, events or locales is entirely coincidental. This book is sold subject to the condition that it shall not, by way of trade or otherwise, be lent, re-sold, hired out, or otherwise circulated without the author's prior consent in any form of binding or cover other than that in which it is published and without a similar condition including this condition being imposed on the subsequent purchaser.

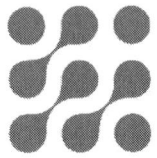

Underbelly Books

Cover photo by Stas Svechnikov & Dmitry Ermakov

For lovers

CHAPTER 1

The old woman never put up a fight. For this reason she has been my favourite victim to date, never once questioning the bitter taste of crushed Atenolol in her tea, or our motives. I'm thankful at least for that much, and by the same token, consumed with pity too.

'Tell me again, Prudence; why do we do this?'

Leaning back in her chair, Prudence says, 'The body will only nourish life if what it desires is the very same. For the few who request salvation, we offer a long-term cure. And we also do it to learn. To help you.'

Looking at the old woman sitting peacefully in the armchair, heart slowing, pulse faint, her life sacrificed to ease my own, reaching salvation demands a much greater pain than that suffered in life. Prudence knows this too.

The old woman is called, Ilse. Ilse's real name is Margaret. Changing the victim's name is Prudence's idea. All of this is Prudence's idea. Detachment: that's what she calls it. To call Ilse by her real name would force me to associate the victim with a life. This is why it's suggested, sorry, I'm instructed, to pick the name of a person I hate, anyone who will force me away from the real person we're about to kill. Ilse Koch was the wife of Karl Koch, commandant of a concentration camp in Buchenwald. Ilse used to remove tattoos from murdered inmates and celebrate torture and obscenity. She was known as the Bitch of Buchenwald. She committed suicide by hanging herself. Margaret's end won't be so quick.

'The most important thing is to be careful,' Prudence says. 'A firm grip on skin this delicate could burst the capillaries beneath, leaving behind finger shapes, a palm print, much the same way a hot hand leaves its mark on a cool window.' Straightening the creases out of her skirt, she adds, 'Any pressure tighter than sock elastic will cause the skin to tear as easily as wet tissue paper. If it looks like there's been a struggle, the police will get suspicious. You understand, Mr Price?'

It's not only the victims who have to have a different name. Today, I am Mr Price. Mr Price was a man who lived on my street when I was a boy. I once saw him beat a dog to death because it shit in his garden. To me he was an evil old man, but to Ilse, he is the kind pharmacist sent to check on her repeat angina prescription, to make sure she's not having any side effects, shortness of breath, palpations and dizzy spells. He has a Master of Pharmacy degree and a wife who's having an affair with her optometrist — Detachment.

Ilse doesn't know these finer details, but they exist if she asks.

Stained glass windows slice sheets of light across Ilse's weathered skin, and I ask Prudence, 'Will there be a struggle?'

Checking her watch, Prudence tells me, 'Doubtful. Ilse's heart is far too weak for that. And far too weak to keep waiting for you.' She picks up the morning newspaper and adds, 'Really, I'm not joking.'

Roll back twenty-two years. I'm seven years old and my mother is having new wall sockets fixed in the house. Three wires poke out of the plaster with exposed copper tips and I'm reaching out to touch them. This is just after she told me an electric shock will paralyze my respiratory system and disrupt my heart causing instant death. I'm seven and she used the word, "respiratory". She went on to say, "Really, I'm not joking."

Prudence is testing me to see if I'm dumb enough to ignore her. She is my accomplice, guardian, authority, and now, my mother.

'It'll be a waste of a perfectly good death, Mr Price,' says Prudence.

Two days before Ilse allowed us both into her house, Prudence told me to learn the correct names and doses of medication pertaining to angina and what might happen to a person if they took too much. The 400 mg of crushed Atenolol Prudence put in her chamomile tea means Ilse's breathing will soon turn shallow. She'll close her eyes for the very last time; little details learnt to prepare me for the inevitable, to help ease my anxieties. Only they're not. If anything, they're making them worse.

Turning another page, Prudence says, 'Stop screwing around and take her wrist. You need this even more than Ilse.'

I move to Ilse's chair. One arm wraps around her neck, the other around the bottom of each thigh. I lift Ilse gently over and slide in beside her.

'Burst capillaries,' Prudence reminds me.

Ilse is a fledgling awaiting its feed. Silvery eyes roll and slip back into her skull. Each sleepy wheeze of her chest brings with it the sickly sweet smell of undigested cake.

Prudence glances at her watch again to tell me I have eight minutes, tops.

Detachment is more difficult than Prudence lets on. New identities are one thing, but every victim has history, one that is made tangible by their environment: the placemats, tea sets, ornaments and photographs. To the side of me, four matching gold-plated photo frames sit on top of a television set, each captive face baring some resemblance to Ilse. The young boy in the school uniform, he has the same sloping brow. The girl with train tracks running over crooked teeth, her chin is pinched together to form a similar dimple. The fat man holding the balloon, he has the same cockeyed nose. The woman in the blue dress has the same thin lips.

Ilse has family.

'I make that seven minutes,' says Prudence.

I snap on a pair of latex gloves, the noise momentarily detracting Prudence from the newspaper. She watches as I lift Ilse's left wrist away from the rainbow blur of colours coming in from the stained glass window.

'What can you see?' she asks.

'Tiny pools of white under the skin.'

'High cholesterol,' she says returning to the paper.

While tracing fingers along green blue veins, I ask Prudence, 'D'you think Ilse ever pressed a knife against her wrist?'

Flicking pages, Prudence replies, 'Never allow emotion to cloud purpose. Now, turn the palm side of her hand face up.'

'I'm not,' I tell her.

'You are, and you're wasting time,' she says. 'Listen.'

Under the strain of death, Ilse's breathing sounds more like bathwater draining into a plughole, a noise which forces me to reconsider why I am here.

But I'm not here. Isn't that the point?

I'm Mr Price who has a two hundred and fifty thousand pound house overlooking the New Forest. A two-year-old baby boy called, Joshua. I'm Mr Price, formerly Mr Alderman. Mr Alderman had a two-bed apartment in the city. No wife. No baby. He was also the guy who ran over my foot in his car when I was thirteen, forcing me to spend that whole summer in the house with my mother.

These names are ways from having to deal with the severity of the kill, to get me through to the next step. To keep me focused. Purpose. They are there to stop me from realising I am committing murder in an attempt to understand my own death.

'You need to place your index and middle finger on Ilse's wrist,' says Prudence, 'about one inch below the base of her hand.'

I wait for reassurance, similar to the first time we did this with Mr Sanderson. I renamed Mr Sanderson to Mr Ripley after Prudence's cat. I hate her cat. In the wake of overdosing on antidepressants, Mr Sanderson/Ripley began convulsing violently on the floor. As calm as a sleeping snake, Prudence turned to me and said, "You have to remember that for the lonely, tomorrow always seemed better yesterday."

Prudence believes this is more than euthanasia, more than thinning the numbers. More than self-therapy. What we do holds reason. I wait for that reassurance and reason, but all I hear is the death rattle.

Prudence says, 'Press your fingers down in the groove between Ilse's middle tendons and the outside bone.' She flicks over the page of the newspaper. 'You should feel a throbbing,' she says. 'Count the number of beats for ten seconds, then multiply this number by six. You'll have her heat rate for a minute. By now it should be less than ten beats per minute. If it's higher, I'll make more tea.'

I can't feel anything. I tell Prudence this and she places the newspaper down and joins me on the arm of the chair.

Slipping out of each black court shoe, Prudence tucks her left foot behind Ilse's back and the other under her thigh. The move makes her dispense uniform ride up a little, high enough to reveal the rabbit's tail of white underwear between her legs. Prudence takes hold of my two fingers and leans towards me.

'You need to savour those last few beats,' she says in a whisper. 'Her death serves no purpose if you don't.'

The main tendon feels hard and rubbery, similar to the flex on a kitchen kettle. We both search the valley between the tendon and the wrist bone.

Prudence whispers, 'Mr Price, concentrate.'

I press on Ilse's skin. A path of blanched skin expands against the grey. Prudence's lungs dip and rise; breasts lifting the pleats from her uniform.

'Concentrate,' she repeats.

I look to the old woman, see her face searching for God in the ceiling.

Prudence fingers release from mine and move between her legs. Her skirt rides up to reveal more of the patterned lace of black stockings.

With eyes half-closed, Prudence says, 'I'm wet.'

This never happened with Mr. Sanderson.

Ilse and Prudence are now struggling for equal breaths, eyelids trembling in unison, both whispering similar noises, poles apart in life and death, yet both so alike at this moment it's hard to differentiate between those caught on the threshold of death, and those getting off. I try to remain focused, clearing my mind of history and heart. But all I hear is Prudence. All I see is her index finger working the channel between her legs.

I close my eyes and remind myself of all her teaching. Soon Ilse's eyelids will stop flickering. The pained gargling noise pulling at my conscience will finally trail off into her very last sigh. Her body will grow cold and blood will settle and rest. And when it does, I will be closer to knowing that when I die, it won't be so bad. Death is the respite of worry. Death is the ultimate Prozac. But before this happens, Ilse and I must endure Prudence's voice once more, its tones flimsy under the weight of arousal, conviction lost to thirst. One word now hangs suspended over us, the last word Ilse will hear, and one that will haunt me long into the night.

'Coming,' Prudence says close to her ear. 'Coming.'

CHAPTER 2

The hospital before me is a reminder that a much greater pain exists outside the world Prudence has created for me. I watch sick people enter through its doors knowing many will never walk out again. This nineteenth-century Victorian building is their potter's field, the bone yard. Their God's acre. Prudence once told me that hospital staff spend so much time around death they actively distance themselves from patients. Befriending any of the sick means you run the risk of them becoming a person, a real person who may bring sorrow when they die. Prudence's cold-heartedness towards Ilse's death is because as a pharmacist's assistant, she has learnt to turn off concern and compassion to protect herself. For Prudence to be successful in her job, she has to be callous.

Pulling into the ambulance bay, I ask, 'Have you ever thought of transferring to another hospital?'

'Why?' Prudence asks, checking the contents of her bag.

'The victims are piling up; surely someone is going to start asking questions soon.'

'And why does that bother me? My job is to give out medication. What the patient does with that medication is up to them. Do you really think the police are going to start questioning a person doing their job?'

Pulling out a small brass clasp and clipping back her hair, she says, 'Besides, I like this place. It brought us together, didn't it?'

I nod.

Prudence places a piece of cotton wool no bigger than her

thumb inside her mouth. Packing it tight into the space between her teeth and right cheek, she turns to me and gives me a big smile.

'Too much?' she asks sipping at each vowel.

Spend enough time looking at the same face and what you think is beauty is nothing more than familiarity. Intimacy erases all the imperfections. Gone are the dark lines under Prudence's eyes. Gone is the slight indentation to the bridge of her nose. I don't even notice the ear that juts further out than the other. Gone too is the small scar above her right eye and the intimidation I once felt in her company. All I see now is hair the colour of polished onyx and wonderfully blue ecliptic eyes. All I see is my salvation.

'It's perfect,' I say.

She pulls down the sun visor and checks herself in the little vanity mirror. In my mind I outline the contours of her profile, every curve of her nose and flick of lip and eyelash. When my heart fails, which it will, I want this image to be my last.

'It is perfect,' she says to her reflection.

The cotton is subterfuge, a trick to convince her boss the root canal took longer than expected. Prudence says getting time off during work hours is almost impossible without a viable excuse. Though Prudence leads me to believe her boss is a real ball-breaker, I know if she feigns a headache he'll wilt like a Valentine rose in March. Prudence is good at manipulation. She's made me an accessory to murder.

'A smack in the jaw will make the swelling look even more convincing,' I say, but she doesn't hear me, or chooses not to.

She leans over and kisses my cheek. The warm flush of blood to my face causes me to look out my side window. The last thing I need is Prudence thinking I'm nothing more than a love-sick fool. If she sees me blush, or notices the corners of my mouth curl due to a fleeting relapse into hope, hope that one day we might be together, lovers in every sense of the word, I might as well crack open my chest right now and pull out my heart for her to trounce upon.

'You're so god-damn-yummy,' she says to the side of my face.

I turn back and she's half way out of the car, her skirt riding up again to reveal the marble of thigh flesh above her stockings. To a great extent, I spend the next few seconds trying to quash a tremble that's developed behind my chest. When it comes to tremors or fluctuations in my heart, I have found the only way to regulate my heartbeat is to conjure up the most horrid scenes of depravity my mind can muster.

Tugging at her skirt, Prudence says, 'Wrap up warm if you go see your father. They're predicting strong winds.'

'You and I spend too much time surrounded by death,' I say, and in my mind, I render the image of a six-inch carving knife scoring a panda's throat.

'You want me to stop helping you?'

'Maybe.'

Pulling out a small handkerchief from her pocket, Prudence leans back in the car. Licking one end she gently rubs my cheek in small circles. The smell of her saliva reminds me of sour milk.

'You have my lipstick on your cheek,' she says, slurring.

I look down the top of her uniform. Each half crescent of each half breast tucked within the black cobweb of her brassiere rattle like alabaster maracas. Towards the centre of each cup is the leopard's spot of each nipple. She catches me looking at her chest, stops rubbing my cheek and moves close enough so her lips almost touch mine.

'You have such wonderful skin,' she says.

Wild horses behind my chest.

I pull away and inform her she needs to purchase mints.

Removing herself from the car, Prudence turns to me and asks, 'Your place? Later?'

She is so casual, so at ease with everything. Less than an hour ago we were both conspirators and executioners in what was ending an old lady's life. For better or for worse, in sickness and in health, Prudence and I are connected by a marriage of expediency, of death and liberation. Most people would still be reeling from such an act, questioning whether or not they left a trail of evidence that would lead the police back to them. Not Prudence. She treats what we do no different from having her nails done or booking a theatre reservation.

I flip the boot and shrug.

Prudence gets out and walks to the back of the car. When I see she's retrieved the plastic big liner containing all the items we touched at Ilse's, I lean over, slam the passenger's door shut and screech towards the main exit. In my rear-view mirror, the faint tumbled image of Prudence's willowy figure is pulled back into the horizon. I place my hand on my chest and those wild horses have stopped galloping.

CHAPTER 3

I stand on Edward Price. A few steps forward and my heel scuff's Daniel Crabtree. Past the colonial angel etched from stone with the words Go to Hell sprayed on in black paint, I stand on a Miriam Lonsdale, Alfred Sycamore and James Thompson. Each headstone below me is identical: four-foot in length and two-foot in width, all forming a pathway leading to the old church overlooking my hometown.

Refteth the body of Constance Aldermen, who departed this life the 10th day of May 1743 in the 61st year of her age.

This is what it says next to my size tens.

I take a few steps more and read: My flefh shall reft in hope to rife wakened by his powerful voice.

Poetic words of death.

The wind picks up making hard work of every step. Every gust feels like a scorned woman's palm against my face. Pulling the collars of my jacket up to shield my ears, I lean into the gale and head towards my father's grave.

Joseph Glass.

This is not his final resting place. There is no coffin desecrated by wood rot, no corpse riddled by worms beneath six-feet of damp soil. The headstone that stands erect from the sodden earth bearing his name, and my grandfather's, is nothing more than a lie — a fake. The inscription is true; Joseph Glass was a beloved father to his only son Jack and daughter Anne Marie. But everything else is fabricated, all done to save me from the same madness that befell him, one brought on by the knowledge that no male member of the Glass family has lived beyond the age of thirty due to a rare heart condition. I'm twenty nine years old. My birthday is less than three weeks. That truth sent my father crazy. For me, it's made me into a serial killer.

I was told my father's body was cremated and scattered along the Bay of Biscay when I was aged five, and though there is an absence of bones in the ground, this plot has become the only place I can truly feel close to him. This gravestone is no different to any cross suspended in a church; it is a symbol, a reminder that things were once different, and that with a little faith, things will be better once again. I draw my finger over the J in his name. I whisper that I miss him, but my words are lost to the wind, a wind that shows no sign of slowing. I decide to make short the visit. Before leaving, I replace a few scattered flowers back into two matching urns with Dad written in gold. I place my hand on the granite headstone, wish him my best, and head back towards my car.

Approaching two wrought iron gates that divide the road from the churchyard, I see an old man tugging at some bunting entangled in a nearby tree. Save for the white dog collar pressing against alabaster skin, he is dressed from head to toe in black.

I shout over to the priest, 'Hell of a day!'

Probably a poor choice of words considering his vocation. The priest's forehead bears down on a pair of wonderful pale green eyes. I try to reassure him with a smile.

'Need a hand?' I ask looking at the bunting.

'Maybe,' he says loosening his expression, 'More than my faith is being tested here.'

Faith. With a little of it, things will be better once again.

I climb the first few branches of the tree to unhook the bunting and coil it around my wrist. Once it's free, I climb back down and hand it over to the priest. By way of thanks, he asks me if I would have a drink with him in the rectory. The wind has blown through his bones and only a brandy or two can thaw the cold residing there. I reflect for a moment on the alternative, the hours spent planning the details of my death, and the despondency that is all consuming. I never cared for brandy but I agree because the line between life and death is threadbare, and to spend just a moment nearer God may strengthen my chances of seeking a reprieve.

'Tell me what you remember of your father,' says the priest, filling my glass three fingers high.

He sits back down and I tell him about one summer many years ago: the sky was a blue bed sheet backlit by a thousand watt bulb. I was wearing short pants, green, heavy knit with loose twine curling out like bedsprings on an old mattress.

'Laughing', I tell him. 'I remembered laughing, but not mine. Someone else's.' I take a sip from the glass, swallow, and add, 'I was playing outside the old maisonette building where my grandma lived. Four teenage boys approached. One of them was carrying a ball of grey wool. Another boy, a red-faced kid, kept saying the same thing over and over: two birds with one stone. Two birds with one stone. In his hand lay a different ball of grey wool.'

'Pigeons?' asks the priest.

I swill the brandy around the sides of the glass tumbler momentarily lost in its contents.

'Yes,' I reply. 'Pigeons. The two boys carried each one to the corner of the maisonette. The birds must have sensed something was going to happen because no sooner were they on the ground each tried flying away, but their wing was broken. From where I was stood, you could just make out the good wing still flapping like crazy.'

The brandy warms my lips.

'They penned the birds in at the corner of the building, trapping them against the wall. A flash of grey and white, sometimes, the perfect black bead of an eye — that was all I saw between the legs of the boys.'

I then invite the priest to remember those old movies where two children would be sat on a bed and one would hit the other with a pillowcase. I ask him he remembers how those pillowcases would burst open filling the room with a snow blizzard of feathers. He nods.

'It was just like that,' I say. 'A snow blizzard.'

The snapping of bone, the squelch of pummelled flesh, the candle wax tear of blood streaming down the pavement, I left all that out. Though important to Prudence, there are some details best left veiled.

'The pigeons, did they hold some greater significance do you think?' asks the priest.

I humour him, pause a second, and then shake my head.

'Then what does such a brutal killing have to do with your father?' he asks.

'My father must have heard me yelling for the boys to stop. He must have heard me crying. I remember he came rushing out of my grandma's and dragged those boys away. It was too late to save the pigeons, but he made sure those boys would do nothing like that again. When he finished, his hands were red raw. He turned to me and I remember his head blocked the sun like a perfect eclipse. A silhouette, a giant shadow man with shoulders as wide as door arches. He carried me into my grandma's lounge. I never forgot that day. It's probably the only time in my life I felt truly safe.'

Past the mullion windows faded with age, the sun creeps into the graveyard. Grey clouds dissolve like soapsuds within the sky. The wind, unremitting in its attack on the panes of glass, causes me to appreciate the priest's hospitality and reflect unfavourably upon the short walk back to my car.

With a face stretched wide with either bemusement or revulsion, the priest asks, 'And that's all you remember of your father?'

Nod.

The priest rubs both hands together as if warming them by a fire not there. The pallor that left him stone-coloured has withdrawn; his face now ruddy, lips cherry red.

'I grew from infant to man in the presence of my father,' he says, 'and I haven't visited his grave in over twenty years.'

I want to tell the priest not to feel so bad; that my father's grave is empty and the only reason I turn up is out of habit. I wish to tell the priest too that I'm due for my own plot soon, maybe next to my father's, or even within the same grave, considering there's enough room. But I don't. It wouldn't do either of us any good to hear these facts said aloud. Too, the consequences of where the conversation would arrive might render me both unhinged and psychotic in the eyes of the old man. Aside from raising awkward questions, being privy to such information may place the priest in a moral quandary. At the end of the day, I am a man hiding a terrible truth.

'It's an admirable quality,' he says, 'loyalty to one you knew very little of.'

I take another sip of brandy. It burns my lips.

'If you don't mind me asking,' he says, picking at a loose

eyelash, 'would you care for anything to eat?'

People look at me and assume I have malnutrition. They see the bones forcing themselves through the skin on my face and without deliberation assume I have bulimia or anorexia. No matter how well I present myself with a shaved face, or clean attire, having a lesser appetite than most consistently mires me from looking respectable.

I lower the glass and shake my head.

'I don't wish to pry, you understand? It's just you look so...'

I wait for: exhausted. Under the weather. Decomposing.

'Weary,' he finally says.

All this sounds too familiar. To know this is not a dream, or an echo of a dream, I pinch the skin around my thigh until the pain becomes unbearable. When I look up again the priest sits with a concerned expression.

'I've offended you,' he says. 'My temperament has always swayed towards the interest and well-being of others. It's not something I can turn off easily.'

I knock down the contents of the glass in one, causing me to cough and gasp.

Without a second thought he hands me a box of tissues from the table next to him and says, 'It's like therapy, I guess.'

I take a tissue.

'Visiting for all these years,' he says. 'It helps fill the void only a father can leave behind.'

Dandruff-sized pieces of tissue fall at my feet as I rub it against my chin.

'At some point, however, every man needs guidance, just like Jesus from His Father'

I want to laugh at his ham-fisted slant to wax lyrical of the Lord's great challenges, but I don't want to offend him either. It's not his fault he sees in me a lamb, someone needing support, nurturing and deliverance. To him I am potential recruit to his congregation; another soul to save. Isn't that the way of the church? Isn't it when you have no hope that they instil the virtues of the Testament? Isn't when you're so close to death they make you believe Jesus is your saviour and only way to the Light? I'm sorry, but I have seen death firsthand, and where I'm going, Christ the Lord Our Saviour won't be the tour guide.

'If ever you're here, visiting your father, and you need to talk, come see me. Don't concern yourself of the time. My door will always be open.'

I wipe the remaining tissue from my lap, thank the priest for his generosity, and commend him on his choice of brandy.

Lifting myself from the chair, I say, 'I have an important meeting I must get to. People are relying on my being there. If I don't make it, I may lose my job.'

This is a lie.

I quit my job a week back. Failed to turn up is a much better explanation. If only to tie up financial loose ends before I die, I should go back and ask my boss to forward any outstanding wages to my home address.

The priest and I are both on our feet. We shake hands and he shows me to the door. Beyond its divide the wind is a Japanese supersonic train.

Walking towards the church gates, over a Dorian Burns and a Reginald Saxby, I shout to the priest that I'll take into consideration his offer should things get too much for me, but each word is lost in a flurry of loose leaves bearing course towards the grey sky above us. The priest cups a hand to his ear. I repeat the sentence, but no matter how much power I instil in each throat-tearing scream, the priest fails to hear me. I am a ghost like the many that roam the gravestones around me; sometimes seen but never heard.

CHAPTER 4

In front of me is a girl bent over. No knickers. Her hands spread apart two arse cheeks the colour of uncooked pastry. The left cheek has the letter T written on in magic marker, the other the letter M. I flick the lever up and a tiny motor kicks in. There's a short mechanical whirl before it stops again, exposing the girl pulling the cheeks of her arse so wide her arsehole opens up into the vowel she wanted. In that new photograph is the word she was trying to produce: ToM. At the base of her spine, written in magic marker are the words: Happy Birthday.

I've seen plenty of these, some more inventive than others. Most women just spray whipped cream across their tits or dress in sexy lingerie and hold up placards. On the odd occasion the soft pale skin of a freshly shaved vagina will bear child-like well wishes written in multi-coloured pen.

Flicking the lever again I see a school's graduation party, pictures of skyscrapers in New York City, an Indian child's fifth birthday. Every so often, a blur of pink forces me to stop the machine and back it up. More often than not it's a holiday snap taken too close on the beach, a burnt thigh, an arm, nose. But it's best not to assume. Seldom does a month pass that I'm not privy to the general public's clandestine urban perversions, those moments never mentioned at the dinner table. I'm the person who knows your mother and father are seasoning their sex life with mail order products, the cock rings, the Astroglide, the amyl nitrate. I know about your sister's drunken striptease for her boyfriend. I've witnessed your brother documenting the size of his penis. I'm the person no one expects exists. But I do.

When I first gained employment at Colour Inc, a photography laboratory in the Eastbridge Industrial estate close to my home, nobody told me it was my job to censor all this filth. Here they have regulations which need to be adhered otherwise the company could lose their developing license. I never saw these regulations. Nobody ever pointed them out. There's no formal discussion relating to crotch shots, no pamphlet on best practice for editing out hard-ons. Middle management handles the subject the same way parents handle telling their kids about sex; they hope someone else saves them the embarrassment. The problem was no one told me jack shit. It was only when an old couple came in to pick up their fiftieth wedding anniversary pictures, and instead received photographs involving a large Samoan man and two overly willing teenage girls, that my boss finally approached me.

"You know it's against company policy to allow an erect penis through to dispatch, right?" said Desmond.

I nodded as if I knew what he was talking about.

"Flaccid only. And a woman's vagina can't be parted. Closed curtains, you understand?"

Nod.

"Just make sure the batch numbers correspond with the address before handing them over to the Sorters, okay?"

Desmond could have fired me, but he didn't. Perhaps this had to do with the high volume of orders we were receiving due to my lack of understanding developing protocol. Or maybe because he just felt sorry for me. People look at me and see someone with no direction, no future. They see redemption.

I left the priest and came into work early with the intention of justifying my recent non-attendance to Desmond. He was nowhere to be found. Instead, Mick, the floor manager, was sat in Desmond's chair. Mick is heavyset with a face better suited behind nylon tights than white-collar work. There are times I feel intimidated by him. He likes that power over people. I find most people like Mick are not generally violent but insecure. They shout a lot and flex their authority because it gives them a sense of self-purpose and control. They were probably bullied as a child by an older sibling. Middle management is their way of revenge. I knocked on the office door and he motioned me in with his hand. I found him pounding a computer keyboard like it was on fire. He didn't look up from the screen, but a short grunt of recognition gave me the confidence to begin the conversation.

"Desmond around?" I asked.

"Can you see him?"

"Can you pass on a message?"

No reply.

"He's probably noticed already, but I've not been in for over a week," I said. "A severe cold, borderline pneumonia."

"Know anything about audit control?" he asked, indifferent towards my confession.

"No."

He pressed his face up against the computer monitor.

"Know anything about Excel?"

"No."

"Piece of shit!" he screamed at the screen.

I asked him if he knew where Desmond was, and slamming his hand against the desk, shouted back, "What arsehole ordered seventy litres of fucking hydroquinone?"

I left the office shortly thereafter and returned back to my car. For a few moments before leaving the premises, I pondered on my newly acquired freedom. Mick was not concerned about me leaving, and I could only assume, considering I had no correspondence or notification of a possible breach of contract, that Desmond cared little for me too. With no job to go to, and so much extra time ahead of me, I was presented with the challenge of filling the day productively before Prudence finished in six hours. For that, I needed another distraction. Fifteen minutes passed. Then twenty. I projected to the day ahead, the weeks, the hours. Time became a vast pit of empty days, on planning for the inevitable heart attack, of writing a will and sorting of personal affects. Thirty minutes passed in a blink, save the last, for this hung in the air like the last drop of water clinging from a faulty tap. It was not long before I found myself sat once again at my desk at Colour Inc.

My job title is Grader. I make sure you're aware that each picture you take, the one where it looks like your uncle Henry has angel wings, is actually light leaking into the camera. For this I stick an Advice Label over Uncle Henry's face that says: FOGGING. When your child looks overly jaundice, I put a sticker on them saying: OVER-EXPOSED. It's my job to point out your ineptness at taking pictures, to spoil the one moment you can't get back.

I flick the lever up on the grading desk and see a baby's first smile, a father and son's fishing trip. These are somebody's happiest moments, things they'll keep forever pressed and protected. And for some stupid reason, seeing other people happy provides the distraction I need.

CHAPTER 5

Prudence presses the REPEAT button on the stereo remote, and for the third consecutive time, Nashville style guitar strumming fills the room. Tapping her thumb on the volume, I hear Mick Jagger reminisce about childhood living. This song is Prudence's way of expressing her feelings to me, sweet harmonious notes carrying other people's words because she is too emotionally isolated to form them herself. The chorus starts up, bass and drums collide. In her own unique way, Prudence is telling me wild horses wouldn't drag her away from me. Prudence has played this song to me three times in a row, all because I asked her if she was seeing her boss. I have no grounds to base this suspicion on. Prudence has never spoken about her boss in a way that suggests she fancies him, or he fancies her. But his name has been mentioned on more than one occasion, and for that reason, I am left paranoid and jealous.

Roll back to this morning, the impromptu wank on Ilse's couch, and how close she got to me before getting out of my car. It's been a long time since I've been with a woman, but I'm pretty sure she was giving off signs. Either that or Prudence wants me dead too. She knows the risks should I get too excited. This relaxed approach towards knocking people off is a trait that concerns me, and I have wondered how far it stretches beyond the patients we visit, and if she sees me as only another potential victim. I hope I'm wrong. I hope that beneath our transgressions lie a deep-rooted attraction, a brooding love that connects us in more ways than death alone. But if my shyness towards returning her advances is forcing her to look elsewhere, then what can I do? I don't own her. I don't even really know her that well. If she wishes to sleep with other men because she can't engage physically with me, then what right do I have to question her? The irony is, she consumes my heart, and yet it's my heart that is forcing us apart.

Prudence removes a damp flannel from my head, the same flannel I placed there ten minutes earlier to help appease a throbbing headache. She goes to the kitchen to rinse it under the tap.

She calls out, 'I never saw such a tidy and clean kitchen, least not for a man.'

When she returns, the cold from the flannel, and the thought of how many kitchens belonging to ex-lovers she has seen, makes worse the pain.

'Is it still hurting?' she asks. 'Maybe you should have another aspirin?'

Watching strangers with cocktail drinks in hand, young girls dressed in pretty white dresses receiving their first holy communion, middle-aged tanned couples holidaying in the south of France, or women shoving cucumbers inside them, has its downsides. The grading desk where I work has two large spools either side of a large angled desktop. One spool holds a roll of uncut photographs. The other collects the same roll of photographs once they've been censored, or had Advice Labels added. The speed at which each picture travels past my eyes makes most of the images a blur. It's impossible to try to follow the detail, even at the lowest speed. The majority of my working day requires me to centre my eyes in one fixed position and adjust my focus only to the stream, not the detail. But there are times when, through a lapse of concentration, or being drawn in by the hypnotic blur of colour, my eyes shift erratically from side to side. With only two breaks during the day, one ten minute coffee break and thirty minutes for lunch, the prolonged exposure to movement feels like I have undergone seven hours in a gruelling NASA G-force simulator. A small price to pay for the luxury of distraction.

'I'm fine,' I say. 'It'll pass soon enough.'

I tell Prudence that we need to talk, that it's very important to me that she listens.

'Sounds interesting.'

I close my eyelids and say, 'It's understandable, what you did next to Ilse this morning.'

'Huh?'

'Touching yourself.'

Silence

'And I'm not bothered about you screwing your boss. I am resigned to the fact my hesitancy in all matters concerning sex will lead to you to seek gratification elsewhere.'

I feel her hand stroke my face. The room is dark. Less light means less head aggravation. I also read that dark colours don't show up stains. It's important to me that everything is clean. Everything I own is either brown or black. The couch we're sat on is chocolate-coloured cotton with black palm tree print; the walls, russet with a chevron weave; the bookcase, a dark mahogany. The flannel on my head is a darker shade of beige. That same flannel now partly obscures my view of Prudence, but I can see enough to know she's looking at me the way people look at cancer victims or babies with Down's syndrome.

'You think I'm screwing my boss?' she asks.

Through the beige mesh, her face is broken into a hundred tiny brown squares, each one revealing an expression pinched by distrust and uncertainty.

'I'm just saying, I wouldn't blame you.'

'Have you seen him? Give me some credit.'

'Well, if not him, anyone. I figure you have needs, which were evident this morning, and if I can't fulfill you in that department, I see no harm in you getting it elsewhere.'

I'm dying inside.

'You mean like some random guy, or girl, at the bar?'

Girl?

'If it helps,' I say.

'What is this?' she asks. 'I thought we had a good thing going on here? Now you want me to go fuck some random person to make you feel better?'

'No, that's not what I'm saying. I just don't want you to miss out.'

'Miss out?'

'If you need to have...'

'Sex?'

'Exactly.'

'Do you want sex?'

Do bears shit in the woods?

'I can't because of —'

Prudence cuts me dead, 'Your heart, I get it. But if your heart was fine, would you want to have sex with me?'

This is the first time we've entered into a conversation where I have admitted to wanting more than just a friendly kiss on the cheek. I've imagined this conversation many times, rehearsed it while sat on the toilet or driving towards work. There would be a timid exchange, a moment where we hesitate before unfettering our feelings towards each other. Prudence would accept my words as though they were wedding vows, and I, with dry mouth and heavy breath, would admit that if the world were to ever fall apart, we would remained together, glued by a mutual respect and love.

Instead, I clam up. Silence.

Prudence flicks the OFF button on the remote and the stereo's lights fade. Through the flannel I watch her move over to her bag, hips swinging out with each step, snapping to the side so her arse drops down and up again. The way it moves reminds me of a leopard's shoulders, the drop and rise preceding a kill.

'Ilse's stuff has gone,' she tells me. 'In case you were wondering.'

I have wanted to know this since Prudence arrived over an hour ago, but the fool who juggles my common sense decided Prudence's supposed infidelity a more important question than discovering if the hospital's incinerator disposed of all items connecting us to Ilse's death.

'Oh,' I say.

Prudence sashays back with a piece of paper. I tilt my head up so my eyes can see.

'You've heard me talk of Mr Davidson?' she asks holding out the paper.

I begin searching the inventory of names and conversations we've had about Prudence's pill popping clientele.

'He's a manic on Prozac,' she says.

I'm none the wiser.

'It doesn't matter. He's due his next repeat prescription. The fifteenth of every month, which is in three days time.'

Prudence pushes out the paper. I know what's on it without even looking. Three days before I met Ilse, Prudence handed me a shopping list containing her address and medication.

I imagine what we do is comparable to being a spy, receiving top-secret information, committing it to memory and then burning it. Unfortunately, that's where all comparisons begin and end.

'Maybe this isn't such a good idea so soon after Ilse,' I say.

Prudence places the piece of paper in her pocket and sits beside me.

'You worry too much,' she says putting her hand on mine. Stroking my knuckles, she adds, 'You'll take a look, at Mr Davidson?'

I shrug.

'Think about what you've learnt so far. Is it really enough to stop you from fretting about your own death?'

I remove the flannel from my forehead and ask her for the piece of paper. When she pulls it from her pocket, I take it.

'There'll be a time when all this will stop,' she says softly. 'You'll be free and I'll be doing the same old shit.'

Prudence's eyes are two perfect blue ceramic beads lost in a shallow rock-pool.

'Loneliness will be my end,' she says.

For a long time we hold each other, watching the corners of the room grow rich and opaque as night crawls into each. Which one of us fell asleep first, I'm unsure, but when I awoke in the morning, beside me was an empty space, save for the details of our next victim. Above the word Prozac was a lipstick impression of Prudence's lips.

CHAPTER 6

The woman with the engagement ring stuck on her finger, the same who smells like the inside of hamster cage, is no different from the woman I met yesterday morning, except the woman yesterday sliced the tip of her finger off while cutting a grapefruit in half.

Holding a chequered tea towel containing ice is the fat woman's husband. He looks a lot like the grapefruit woman's husband, only thinner. Each time the tea towel touches his wife's finger, which looks more like a donkey's dick, the woman winces and the husband looks to me and rolls his eyes. This is what the grapefruit woman's husband did. This is their way of initiating a conversation, and as such, this is what I've come to expect every morning while attending the Accident and Emergency ward of Willow Bank Hospital.

'Why she thought it would still fit after all these years is beyond me,' he says before turning back to his wife. 'What made you think it would fit you after all these years?'

I pretend to watch the small wall-mounted television. The news is playing. An attractive reporter with a fine pair of legs and white teeth is telling me about a young girl in Florida who was taking pictures of nurse hound sharks, black tip reef sharks, and tiger sharks from a bridge in a zoo for fish. The picture on the screen reveals one half of the bridge submerged in a lagoon, the other is clinging tightly to the embankment. A piece of engineering as volatile as a rope bridge suspended over perilous waters inhabited by sharks seems like an oversight by the architects, but the news reporter seems more concerned about the welfare of the child than any design flaw.

'She was going to give it to our son,' says the fat woman's husband.

I'm half listening while watching the pretty reporter point at the lagoon. Fingernails of cherry red.

'His girlfriend's expecting. I told him he better leave her, or marry her. But he's always been a little soft in the head.'

I didn't need to hear the rest. Anyone with half a brain could figure out the son had approached his mother about his intentions, and she had looked around in her jewellery box at home and found an old ring she hadn't worn for years, one roughly the size needed for the boy's girlfriend. Seeing that ring had reawakened a memory in her, a memory of when her husband was a more compassionate lover, when flowers were bought on a whim, and not after an argument. Whatever. The ring represented a better time so she slipped it on. All that probably happened an hour ago.

I hear a whimper force its way out the woman's mouth.

'Shame you're straight love, you'd make a great lesbian with a finger that thick.'

The sound of laughter causes me turn away from the television and over to the husband. His face is a crumpled up wino's booze bag. The noise out of his mouth is a petrol lawnmower running out of juice.

A few seconds is all it takes before his laughter attracts the attention of everyone else sat waiting for medical treatment. His face is turning a bluish mauve, not too dissimilar in shade to the fat woman's finger.

I return to the television.

On the screen a little black figure is underwater, white underbellies of sharks circle its head like huge smoke rings. This is the news company embellishing the story with stock footage of a diver feeding the sharks so we get an idea of what this girl saw when she went under the water. The news company is spoon-feeding us tension, forcing us to feel for this girl. I can't feel anything because of this guy's laughter.

The reporter says, 'Luckily for little Riana, the sharks had just been fed…'

And the guy, he just keeps on laughing.

Under normal circumstances, I would walk. But like the article said, I have to think about my heart.

The article.

Roll back three months. I'm sat waiting on more test results at my local GP and I pick up a lifestyle magazine in the waiting room. Inside was an article that presented the findings of a cardiologist, one with over thirty years experience. He articulated the sudden rise of cholesterol levels and obesity due to fast food, and that heart attacks occur mostly during the hours of 6.00AM to 9.00AM. When you've been diagnosed with a rare heart problem, one where fluctuations and irregularities of rhythm could prove fatal, and a specialist with over thirty years training discloses a period where the heart is at its weakest, you sit up and take notice. I took a trip to the public library's medical reference section later that day. In the aptly named book, Affairs of the Heart, the publication provoked more nausea within me, but considerably less scepticism. It appeared to be true; God had allocated three hours in every day when the heart is more likely to stop. I had two choices: either sleep in and risk the chance of being the vile stench lingering in the lobby, and the person the neighbours reflect upon over dinner parties as, "Tragic" and "Unlucky", or make a positive effort to safeguard my future by being around those that could help prolong it. At least here at Willow Bank Hospital I will just be "Ill-fated" a "Victim" or a "Sad loss" when their efforts fail, labels I can live, or die with. So now every morning I awake at 5.00AM. A short drive and I'm sat in the Accident and Emergency ward. Here I wait. I wait three and a half hour until 9.30AM. After 9.30AM, I return home. Call it contingency planning. Or life insurance.

Cultivating patience and calm is paramount during these three hours. I don't want to put unnecessary pressure on my heart. I have also come to realise very little separates each person here. Minutes tick by so very slowly. They hang in the air like sleeping fish. Pain unites each of us, in one guise or another, and it's our search for a means to channel our pain that defines us. How a person copes with tragedy, worry or loss is really the biggest of life's mysteries. But when they do, half the battle is won. The other half is remembering why you want to fight for life in the first place. For the woman's husband, he copes with the distress of seeing his wife in pain by resorting to humour, by making light of the situation. For the woman, she found solace in articulating her emotions not in words, but through tears, by crying in public. I imagine the latter is very liberating.

My own outlet, my own means of coping with life and death, came in the guise of a woman.

Prudence is a distraction against the things I have no control over like the sweaty palms and dry mouth, or worse, the vice crushing pain across my chest. It was sitting here, among the wilted and wounded, when I first saw Prudence walk by in her dispenser's uniform and black court shoes. I saw her every day, a stranger, beautiful and dependable. She was the only constant during the unruliness of my thoughts. Seeing this strange woman every day meant I'd forget about my heart. And if it wasn't for retrieving repeat prescriptions from the hospital pharmacy, instead of taking the long trip to the city, I never would have spoken with her. You could say repeat prescriptions and fate became our cupid.

8.59AM.

I'm looking out for Prudence, my perfect distraction from the woman's husband. Prudence is never late.

I ask the woman for the time, to make sure my watch is correct, and the husband shushes her because he wants to know why it is I'm too good for his joke.

'I didn't find it funny,' I reply.

'Not funny?' he asks.

'It was a little offensive.'

9.06AM and both the husband and I are both on the floor, his hands gripped tight around my throat. He seems determined to hurt me, but by the same token he yells at me to, 'Breathe!' That's what he keeps saying, 'Breathe!' And although I'm trying my best, it's difficult with his hands around my throat.

I stick both thumb pads into each of his eye sockets, all the while conscious of my heart rate. Two security personnel come running down the corridor and separate us. I'm told to leave because the triage nurse has no record of me reporting any illness or complaint. Outside I think I'm going to faint. My heart is a sparrow trying to escape from a shoebox. I sit down on a nearby bench. Next to me is a guy reading a newspaper in a dressing gown. From underneath the gown an IV drip trails out to a bag of clear liquid on a pole with wheels.

He looks up at me and says, 'Your nose is bleeding.'

I wipe it and tell him, 'I just got into a fight.'

He rustles his paper straight and asks if I won.
I pinch the bridge of my nose to stop the bleeding.
'Not too sure,' I say. 'How can you tell?'
'Last man standing. The winner is always the last man standing,' he says.
'Then yes, I'm standing. At least for another day.'

CHAPTER 7

Each bedroom in my mother's house has a period fireplace. None of them work. Within the belly of a few, white church candles that have never been lit gather dust. Pots of potpourri fill the rest. Decoration, my mother calls it. This is what I'd come to expect as normal. Normal is warming your bedroom with electric heaters although a perfectly good fireplace sits there gathering dust. Normal is having candles and never lighting them. Normal is having a heart problem kept secret from you by your own mother. Normal is dishonesty to save you from madness.

Roll back twenty years. Before the blackouts, before the candles and the potpourri, I lived in this house with my mother and older sister, Anne Marie. Back then I found the house stifling. Living with two females has a way of making you dispassionate towards home life. For one, you are always outnumbered when it comes to voicing any concerns; even if there's a valid point you are making, women conspire by default. The communal areas of the house left me feeling more like an interloper than a member of the family too. Flower print wallpaper, cherry reds, pinks, delicate decoration, all these things forced me to detach myself from my home for fear of becoming emasculated. On several occasions I foolishly tried to influence the rooms I spent time in, leaving behind a model aeroplane on the chaise lounge, a copy of 2000 AD next to Marie Claire, newspapers left open at the football fixtures instead of the Agony Aunt letters. No matter what I did, things would soon return to how they were, and I, as if in the wrong for wanting to retain a hold on my masculinity, would receive a few choice words from my mother about discipline and cleanliness. It came to me that the only real affect I could have in the home was to do nothing. Having observed how my friend's fathers acted in their homes, the master of the house had the right to sit on his arse and watch television night and day if he so wished. It was his right too to comment and mock his wife and order her around. While most kids revered football players and dreamt of scoring the winning goal at Wembley Stadium, I was in awe of the simple man, the man who controlled his home, who drank beer indoors and was free to fondle his ball-sack to all and sundry.

I started by spending more time in front of the television wearing just my underwear and adopting an unconcerned manner. Soon my mother began referring to me less and less as her son and more her lazy-no-good-lodger. She'd watch as I lounged around on the couch after school, eating for free and reading comics. And it was while dozing on the couch one day that she woke me and said it was high time I did more around the house. She referred to a long list of chores. My mother said chores were part of being the man of the house. It was a man's job to maintain standards and keep the home safe. I asked her what that meant, "Man of the house", and she said women prefer men who protect them, who provide and sustain a safe environment, not lazy sons-of-bitches who just eat, shit and sleep. The house is a reflection of a man. If it smells, it tells a woman he lacks standards. If the house has damp on the walls, a leaking roof, broken door handles, a woman will assume the man is lazy. She said, "If you ever want to marry a beautiful woman, you'd better shape up, mister."

I thought back to my friend's fathers, their wives. Most were ugly and depressed, skin shiny with sweat, hands reddened through wringing clothes and scrubbing dishes. They were shadows of women and ones you wouldn't wish to spend a great deal of time with alone. My mother's comments stayed with me for many days. I wanted her to be wrong, but the more I thought of the families surrounding our homes, and the women whose husbands didn't work and drank beer all day, I realised she was right — negligence and laziness repelled beautiful women. Anne Marie backed my mother's theory up. Why wouldn't she? If only to abdicate her chores to me, and occasionally, when mother wasn't at home, order me around to clean up after her. So I began to take out the rubbish, clean my bedroom, carry plastic bags filled with food from the precinct to our home. I washed the dishes, vacuumed the carpets, and changed the toilet rolls when they ran out. I did most things, except the laundry. And Anne Marie and my mother, they never lifted a fucking finger the whole time. I began to feel less like a son and brother, and more like a husband, fettered not by love, but instead, dependency.

The other kids at school would tease me, called me names like Cinderella and skivvy. The perfume of my youth was not grass or the syrupy scent of candy, but bleach and Ajax.

Roll on ten years. School is over. I didn't have a job planned, nor did I have any idea what I wanted to do when I left college. A few of the underachievers were talking about working the summer at a company that developed photographs. They said the company were recruiting for new staff. The money wasn't great but the work was easy. I went for an interview the following week and got the job as a Grader. I worked pretty damn hard and put in more hours than was needed. My plan was to get enough money together so I could move out and rent a place of my own, a place where I could come and go when I pleased, one far away from my mother and sister, and more importantly, a place clean enough to bring home beautiful women. With a few extra shifts, I saved enough for a bond and enough for the first month's rent. With every imperfect picture, every perverted snapshot, I was inching forward each day to leaving all my shit behind.

Happiness is fleeting.

After a twelve-hour shift grading pictures I returned back to my mother's home. In the living room were three large pots of canary yellow paint and one brush. There was a hand-written note taped to one of the pots:

This should brighten up my bedroom. I'm staying with a friend for the weekend so have it done before I get back. And open the windows so the fumes from the paint don't get on my chest.

That was it. No please. No thank you. I read the line over again about her, "friend". Friends to my mother were transient arseholes with no fixed address and aching balls. They all shared the same need to fuck her until it got boring, or too serious. Generally it was the latter. There was a phone number to call in case of an emergency. The first set of digits told me it was a business, most probably a hotel.

I didn't paint the bedroom. I lit a candle in her bedroom fireplace instead.

Flames crackled. Dust burnt in sparks of white. The miasma reminded me of the rank bins outside my grandma's maisonette. The flame lived for about half an hour. Had it not been for a dense white smoke that started pouring out from the chimney flue towards the ceiling, it may have gone on for longer. I realised quickly that something was in the flue. I blew the candles out but the smoke kept coming. I reached up into the flue and pulled out a soot-covered wooden box with brass clasp, singed. Inside were the death certificates for my father and my grandfather, all with different dates to the ones both Anne Marie and myself were told. On my father's headstone it says he died in 1977 at the age of thirty-four; my grandfather, 1955 at the age of forty-two. The death certificates stated my father actually died in November 12th 1969 of heart failure at the age of twenty-nine. When I checked my grandfather's, he died in 1946 aged just twenty-eight. Cause of death: heart failure.

There were more death certificates, ones for my great grandfather and his father, old and brown with tatty edges. They both died in their late twenties, both of the same illness that saw off my father.

When my mother returned home from her dirty weekend, I had the box in the centre of the dining table, each certificate lay out in a perfect line above séance hands. She looked at the certificates and then at me. The sluice gates of her mouth opened and a river of shit-steaming abuse poured out. She called me a nosy little bastard and that I had no right looking through her personal things. She grabbed my shoulder. Slapped my face hard. I didn't feel it. The discovery had numbed my body, all senses channelled to the part of my brain where secrets are solved, mysteries unveiled.

The next day I went to see my doctor.

He tested my blood pressure and asked a few questions regards to my well-being. Talk came around to family history. I told him about my father, and grandfather, and the time I was mowing my mother's garden and blacked out.

"Sometimes, when I run up the stairs, I feel faint and a little unsteady on my feet," I said.

He referred me to a cardiologist who ran more tests. They did a blood workup that looked beyond ordinary cholesterol numbers and found an elevated level of Lipoprotein A in my blood. He told me high elevations of Lipoprotein A are linked with heart disease. He used an ECG to check my heart rate and asked about the blackouts. He then made me run a little on a treadmill to determine how long it took before my heart rate returned back to its normal rhythm. In his office, he wrote a repeat prescription for a time-release niacin called Niaspan that helped reduce high levels of Lipoprotein. I was given Atenolol, a beta-blocker/blood pressure control, the same Prudence gave Ilse. Clicking his pen closed he said, "The Atenolol will limit your heart rate and make sure your BP is under control. But please, Mr Glass, try not to exert yourself."

The pills were to help me get through day-to-day living, to make sure I didn't blackout when running for the bus, walking great distances, or sat at my desk watching happy faces and perverted sex acts. The pills were the interim measure. If things got worse, more tightness, more blackouts, I would need an operation. Behind a thousand yard stare, words flew past my ears like arrows: Blockage. Open. Stent. Titanium mesh. Angioplasty Balloon.

There was a conversation. A theory suggested. Can death be predicted? No man with the Glass name had made it past thirty years old. Their hearts were unified by the same imperfection, a limited amount of beats that expire in less than thirty years. I asked him if he thought that was odd, and through heavy breaths and long pauses, with words softened by experience, he told me of a rare and largely unfamiliar disorder of the heart. He explained Sudden Arrhythmia Death Syndrome. He had seen cases where two or three perfectly healthy members of the same family had died suddenly without any warning due to a massive heart attack. It's caused by a thickening of the heart muscles and irregularities in the electrical impulses responsible for the natural rhythm of the heart. This would explain my father's passing and my grandfather and his father before him. I was told to wear a heart monitor for a few weeks. Worst case scenario, they would fit a cardioverter defibrillator that delivers electrical impulses in the absence of normal impulses. I thanked him, declined his offer of the monitor, took my prescription and left.

Roll on a couple of days. A musty hotel room, a place to measure my past and what was left of my future. The headboard from the adjoining room tapped out in Morse code that Darwin was right; the strong will survive and the weak will prevail only in loneliness and death. The veiled light from the windows cloaked the room with a sickly pallor. Fate had driven me to this sepulchre, its walls the backcloth to a dying man's shadow, one weakened and malformed by history. I returned home to speak with my mother. To find out the truth.

A cigarette perished in the time it took her to tell me how every family has secrets, none so grave they reveal when your husband is going to die. My mother lit another cigarette and dragged me back to when she was six-months pregnant with Anne Marie. Grandma Glass came to see her. Grandma Glass lived alone in a small house where time died with my grandfather. To step into Grandma Glass's house is like stepping into post-war Britain. That was her way of coping, to never change the world they both occupied — a world of rationing, bloodshed, fighting and death. The happiest time of her life.

Grandma Glass brought out the box, the same one containing the death certificates that I had found in the flue. With a burning woodbine she exhaled words of misfortune and destiny to my mother.

Listen, she said: The sentry of routine is ignorance.

Remember, she said: Ignorance protects. It saves the heart from pressure and fails to govern the mind with murky thoughts.

Never forget, she added: For any of the Glass men to know the truth would rupture their sanity.

Tears ran down the rivulets of my mother's youthful face, hollowing out cheeks, furrowing eye and mouth...or so she said.

Things change.

Tears dry.

Acceptance came and routine masked the fractures of a deepening truth.

My father showed no signs of fainting, dizzy spells, shortness of breath. Because of this my mother began to believe the condition had skipped a generation. Then, after his twenty-sixth birthday, he began having chest pains, not so bad he fainted, just enough for him to be worried. The doctor found an irregular heartbeat. A pacemaker was fitted. The abdication of truth was too much for my mother to bear alone.

The truth will out, and so did the box with its death certificates.

While I knew hearing the truth behind my heart condition

would be hard, as she spoke of my father's anguish upon knowing his fate, I felt a moment of complete satisfaction. I realised then both he and I shared a similar moment in time, a moment when we were sick, angry and confused. He too must have wanted to walk out of the room, to spend the rest of his time alone without commitment and accountability. And deep down, knowing my mother could see the similarity between us, made me feel closer to him than ever before.

A few months before his thirtieth birthday, my father closed himself off to the world, his wife and children. He began to drink at home. Joseph Glass, the placid, understanding husband, began to hit his wife. Joseph Glass, the friend and father began to go missing for days. My mother asked if I remembered any of this. I shook my head.

Her reason for hiding the box was nothing more than to protect me from the truth: to save my sanity. It was in my best interests that I never know, and that I never marry. She said this. No woman should ever know her husband's fate. No woman should carry that much of a burden.

That night I packed a bag, hopping from one hostel to another before landing a cheap room in a rundown building on the opposite side of town, a place as far away as possible from her home. The landlord reduced my bond on account of the room smelling like a dead person. I asked if a dead person lived here before me and he laughed. I told him it wasn't a joke and he laughed some more. He handed me the key and said the rent would be due the beginning of every month.

Some people say freedom smells sweet. For me it smelt of death.

CHAPTER 8

An old wood-fired cook stove made of black cast iron heats a copper kettle. To boil enough water to make two cups of tea, the priest has to use five small logs, which he throws into a small square hole located directly underneath the hotplates.

Before shutting the stove's heavy iron door, he says, 'In the winter, you won't find a room in the rectory warmer than this,' and I hear the snapping of wood as it succumbs to the fire.

The way the priest moves around the small kitchen gives me the impression he's never been here before. His moccasins shuffle across the linoleum floor in short little bursts, filling the room with the sound of paper being repeatedly torn in half. He opens a cupboard door, stares into it unsure of what might be lurking inside, and then closes it cautiously.

'I'm sure I had some,' he says to me after throwing another peculiar stare inside an overhead cupboard. 'I used it last summer while trimming back the azaleas. I acquired a nasty sting from a nettle bush.'

The wall above where the priest is stood looks the same as the other three, nicotine yellow which was probably once cream that was probably once white.

'That said, a dock leaf is the best cure to temper the sting of the common nettle,' he says.

'Ammonia in urine is good for stings, too,' I reply.

Like Grandma Glass's house, no room in the rectory has changed for at least fifty years. The doors are original from the turn of the century. They're old and warped with scratch marks, and the handles are positioned low down so you have to bend like you're praying in order to turn them. Maybe that's why they're positioned so low. Above the door in the dining room is a wooden box that lists all the rooms. Below each room name is a little window with a star in the middle. Jutting out the bottom of the box is an old bell on the end of a spiral.

While searching the pantry, the priest tells me how each room has a brass button on the wall, and many years ago the parish priest who lost his legs to polio, a Father Cole, would press one of those buttons and the bell would ring lighting up the box. The person responsible, a maid, or carer, would check the box and instantly know where to find the father.

'It was the first intercom system of its type,' he says. 'Revolutionary at the time, some said. Of course it's not worked for —'

The priest produces a half bottle of Witch Hazel from a shelf. He thinks it will help lessen the bruising around my eye. My eye doesn't look too bad. It is swollen, red and weepy, but the priest believes the effects of pain surface long after it has abated.

In the kitchen, the copper kettle whistles like a train.

The priest sits again on a green velveteen chair and asks about the fight. This he does at the exact moment my teeth clasp a piece of shortbread he put out to accompany the tea. I take a bite regardless and he waits until I've finished.

Listening to myself explain the details of the fight with the woman's husband, and how it began, sounds comical. The priest doesn't share the absurdity of the situation as much as me. Even when I let out a little abashed snort towards the end he remains perfectly still, frozen. If not for the knuckle of his index finger brushing against his lips, I would happily declare his passing.

'Does this happen frequently?' he asks me, repositioning his finger to the soft undercarriage of his chin.

'Fighting? No,' I tell him.

'Then why lose your temper with this man?'

There was no short answer. To walk the priest through all matters concerning my heart is a journey best travelled when time is of no consequence. The priest assures me that time and patience remains two elements encouraged in the clergy.

'A priest without either,' he says, 'is like a fish without gills.'

So I begin with my family history, and then move stealthily towards meeting Prudence. I tell him everything, save for the murders. Death to the church is a profitable commodity, but it did not sway my decision to remain mute about Prudence's culling, especially since I saw warmth and compassion toward my current predicament in the priest's face.

'Prudence, she feels the same way about you?' he asks stretching out his feet, the dry twig snap of joints hitting all four walls of the rectory.

'That's what I believe.'

'Good,' he says slowly forcing himself from the grip of the chair.

'You'll have to excuse me, Jack. There is mass to prepare. Of course, you're welcome to stay, but I'm quite sure you could use the time more productively.'

I agree and stand to meet him. Years of greeting mourners and congregation assures a firm but comfortable handshake. He leads me to the door, the shifting of his feet echoing through the rectory like autumn leaves.

Genially he adds, 'I'll offer a prayer to Saint Jude, and the first votive candle lit every morning will be yours.'

Outside the sole of my shoe grazes the name of Grace Fairchild, reminding me that while the eyes of the saints look down upon me, it is the dead I'm closest to.

#

Work.

There is no sign of Desmond again. Mick tells me he's at a meeting and that four rolls of uncut photographs are waiting to be graded. He doesn't even ask about my eye.

Back at the grading station and I push the lever up. Each smiling face I cover up with an Advice Label. Each moment of happiness reminding me of how precious life is and how each moment should be savoured and not wasted, I draw a line through it so they are cut from the final set of prints.

In the car on the way home the steady rhythm of a headache partially closes my left eye. Through a part-squint, the sky beyond the window is packed tight with plumes of reddish clouds as though the heavens have been set on fire. I decide to stop and admire one of a few remaining sunsets left awaiting me.

Four songs in on the radio and the roads are clogged worse than my arteries with people returning home from work. Side streets pass to my left and right. I continue along the road. In the sky, plumes of reddish cloud weaken to Halloween cobwebs that hang across the cold, blue veil of night. Darkness is preparing to overthrow day. The splendour of light soon to succumb to pastel shades. What beauty remains, night will plunder.

I arrive at a pub close to where I live. It has a suitable-sized beer garden and all the benches outside are vacant. The car is parked off a side street so no police can see me get back in.

Inside, a barman with a podgy little face asks, 'You been in a fight, friend?'

I press the swollen flesh around my eye. Before mustering up a smile, I say, 'My son caught me with a tennis racket. He's young and full of enthusiasm, but his backhand is terrible.'

A tight little frown puckers his mouth to arsehole-sized portion.

'I can't be having trouble here, son. You understand?'

I look around the room. Five other people sit slumped in their chairs, backs arched like shrimps. Four of the faces are riddled with age. The last is wheelchair bound. Regardless, I nod my head in agreement. What follows is an uneasy silence marred only by his teeth sucking and my laboured breathing. It hurts my face but I smile again, which finally secures me a drink.

The pint has far too much head, but I don't complain. My headache is burning brighter than the star of Bethlehem. Heading towards the door leading to the garden, the bartender informs me it's locked.

'You can't be taking glass into the garden anyway, son,' he says. 'Plastic pint pots only.'

Everyone is looking at me — at least I think they're looking at me. Perhaps I'm looking at them? It's hard to be sure without making excessive eye contact. I take my drink and find a seat close to a window. This seems to please the bartender and allows him to join an elderly man at the opposite end of the bar. They both release overstated laughter and jeers, the cacophony of sounds akin to the Philharmonic Orchestra tuning up. I look around and nobody else seems bothered by the noise. Most patrons are doing nothing more than staring hopelessly into their drinks. The few talking clearly don't seem at ease with what they're saying. They all appear united by the same frustrations, misery and luck, which judging by their expressions is not of the good kind. God has chosen to paint each with the same brush and muted colour, rendering them in the form of gloom and glazed with a husk of hardship. In truth, the room is inconsolable, and yet within it I find comfort. The more I drink the more I feel cast in similar tones. My posture changes from straighten spine to slump, minutes dissolve away like the hundreds of tiny air bubbles lacquering my glass. The miserable and forlorn, the sots and the rejected, not one stares back if my eye drifts towards them. A strange feeling comes over me, one oddly reassuring, because for the first time in years, I feel a note of acceptance.

CHAPTER 9

The stairwell leading to my flat puts to test every muscle and joint in both legs. I count each one to help take my mind off the pain. By the time I reach twenty-four, my calves feel like two aggravated hornet nests and the blood rushing through them is like soda. Step number thirty-five and I see a leg stripped bare hanging through the balustrade above me. Under the lights of the stairwell it is the colour of meringue. On the end is a black court shoe.

Sitting across the full length of step forty-two, dressed in a long black coat and what seems like nothing else, is Prudence. Mascara bleeds from each eye making her look like a ghoul, the end of each nostril sunburnt red. Upon seeing me, her face betrays any sadness to deliver a smile that lacks any real conviction. Two more steps and we're both in each other's arms, chests beating in perfect rhythm. She casts adrift words within the sea of cotton my coat offers her lips.

When she pulls away she says, 'Your eye?'

I wipe the oil slick of mascara from her cheek and tell her I opened a door too fast earlier this morning. Pallid lips draw towards mine, tear-stained with spices from the sea. It is the consequence of sorrow that prompts our first kiss, and though excited and desperate to reciprocate, in the seconds preceding I am consumed with the understanding that again fate has urged misfortune to bring Prudence and I closer.

Inside my flat.

Prudence makes her way over to the stereo. I ask her if she

wants anything to drink and she tells me something red. In the kitchen the only noise is the hum from the refrigerator and my breathing. The bottle of Merlot shivers as I pour.

Prudence stands in the living room waiting for me, swaying slightly to the first few beats of Chicago's, If You Leave Me Now.

'It's Patrick's fault,' she says.

Patrick is what she calls her boss. To everyone else he's Mr Denshore. With such familiarity, she wonders why I call into question their relationship.

'He said I needn't turn into work if my mouth was still sore after the root canal.'

I expected as much, but even so, his compassion is a cattle prod of electricity to my stomach.

'I was going to meet you, before you left for the hospital, but I fell back to sleep.'

She takes the two glasses from my hands and places them on the small, brown coffee table next to the brown couch.

'I went to the hospital and waited outside for you, but I guess you left. I then drove to your flat and I've been here since, waiting. Where were you?'

Prudence doesn't know about the fight, the conversation with the priest, or that I sat for eight hours playing voyeur into the lives of strangers. Eight hours. To bend and fashion time so days are abridged is a trick for only the lonely to practise. Work compresses my days by a third, and sleep assures the swift arrival of the next day. Without either the hands of a clock will hesitate before continuing. I once fell from the top step of a ladder whilst securing a security light at my mother's home a few years ago. The drop was no more than twenty-feet, but as I descended towards the ground, the distance grew to four times that size, and in turn, time lengthened. The world around me moved at normal speed, but the prospect of being injured slowed time to a crawl. It is the same when I am alone. An hour is built upon the fifty-nine minutes that precede it, yet within my world, an hour can hold up to four times that amount. And yet an hour with Prudence is as fleeting as a solitary second.

Eight hours she has waited for me. For me, that feels like a day.

To make matters worse, I cannot tell her that while she sat alone beside my door, I had been at work. I told her was going back today to quit. Prudence knowing the truth now would make me look like a coward and a liar. I also feel disclosing the fight with the fat woman's husband will only complicate matters further and call into question my dependency on her.

She grabs both my hands, guiding them to her backside where they rest on the precipice of both cheeks.

'I went to a café in the morning and the cinema in the afternoon,' I say. 'I opened the toilet door in the cinema too fast and it caught my eye.'

Over her shoulder the small black convex shape of her arse calls out to me.

She says, 'I was worried something might have happened to you.'

I bring my face into view and shake my head as if dismissing her assumption to be foolish and absurd.

Prudence links her arms around my neck, pushing her head into my chest.

'You okay?' she asks.

The air around us turns to water. The wrench of a thousand leagues contracts my lungs. I draw in a deep breath, then another, and that which was flaccid is now swelling. I'm sure it won't be long before she feels it pressing against her hipbone.

'You're not having an attack, are you?' she asks.

I shake my head, knowing that what little stronghold I have on self-control will relapse into passion, an undertaking that will surely prove more demanding on my heart than my will-power.

Prudence leads me with her hand towards the couch. We sit and she slowly repositions my hand on her chest, just below her left breast.

'I would give it to you if I could. In a heartbeat,' she says.

Against my palm I feel the dull repetitive beat of a healthy heart. In a movie, that line would work. But in reality it seems too rehearsed.

My hand migrates to her breast. In all my fantasising of us being together I never once gave thought to how each would feel. They are small and pert, firm and unyielding to the touch. Much the way a baker influences the shape of bread by kneading the dough, I begin massaging, gently at first and then with more energy.

'I don't understand,' she says.

I answer with a kiss.

The ocean again, the deadwood and the flotsam, then the fusty tang of onions as her tongue hesitantly pushes against mine. The hard stud of her nipple presses into my palm.

She pulls away and asks, 'Are you sure?'

I reach down and lift the hem of her skirt. Her song is the verse of a sigh followed by the chorus of a moan. A violent river rushes under my skin. The noise in my ears is like an aeroplane cabin at thirty-five thousand feet. I pull my hand away from Prudence's and slip it over the waistband. Her head rolls back, face pulled tight with what I'm hoping is pleasure but looks more like constipation. Behind my chest plate, a thousand moths flutter around in search of light. As Prudence nears an orgasm, every part of me shivers. She commands me to keep going, to never stop. I open my eyes and look at her face: cheeks flush, mouth singing a silent opera. Concentration is channelled to my extremities, the balls of my feet, my toes. Both are numb. I remember the article: a lack of oxygen to the heart will turn one's fingernails a bluish purple. Against the weak yellow hue from a small table lamp, all my fingernails look black. This worries me more. Teeth throb as the moths in my chest quadruple in quantity and bash violently the racking of my chest. I hold my breath hoping the cough that swells in my throat will subside, but I panic and begin swallowing at the air around me while still trying my best to retain a degree of rhythmical movement with my fingers.

Prudence's back arches, hands grip whatever soft brown material is close by. Moaning stops and her whole body shudders. Face now locked with an intensity I've never witnessed on a person before. I search for air while still pleasuring her. This is when Prudence starts making noises like someone is strangling her. All this lasts for another twenty seconds before her body is brought back to life by the first post-orgasm breath. I, however, am now reduced to a man stricken with fear, hand clutching my chest, a pain already blistering the bone and flesh within me. The similarity between Prudence's climatic expression and my look of sheer panic must appear similar at this point, though both at opposite ends of the emotional spectrum. I move my hand off her and assume the crash position. There I wait for the Atenolol to cap my heart rate, or the dark mist that pre-empts a blackout.

'You okay?' she asks between heavy breaths.

I feel her hand across my back, rubbing gently in circles.

With her legs ajar, and my head so low down, I'm torn between coping with the pain in my chest and fending off the urge to gawp like a demented fool at her vagina.

'You want me to phone for an ambulance?' she asks. Before I can reply she says, 'I'm going to phone for an ambulance.'

I hear her drop the phone's receiver. Three times she does this before placing the phone back on its stand.

'I'll be fine,' I say. 'It will pass.'

Prudence looks over to me, skin ruddy from the orgasm, two hard-boiled eggs for eyes. She picks up the receiver again and holds it out to me. I notice it trembling. She looks so perfect and vulnerable I want to cry.

'Don't do that shit!' she yells. 'You're telling me you're fine so I won't phone. And then I won't phone and you'll get worse and you'll die because that's what you really want. You want to die!'

If Prudence and I were married, she's the one who would be entrusted not to tell me about my family secret. She's the one who needs to project calm and serenity at all times.

'You want to leave me now, don't you?' she says almost in time with the song still playing.

The resolve in her voice is barely evident under the stress of seeing me suffer. In the months we have known each other, sharing and contributing to mortality, I have never seen her so scared. The first time I witnessed death firsthand, Prudence projected an air of formality that I admired. It would be later, when I began to have feelings for her, that these same attributes closed her off from expressing any emotion towards me other than sympathy. But there is concern now, concern beyond that of a collaborator, a partner and accessory to murder. I'm beginning to think she actually cares for me the same way I do for her. I wiggle my toes and feel a little sensation reach each tip. The moths behind my chest settle: the blood in my veins loses momentum. The pounding from my heart eases to gentle raps. I am overwhelmed by so many things, but none more so than the knowledge that Prudence's fear is the only beta blocker I need.

CHAPTER 10

On my tenth birthday my mother decided she didn't want to risk bringing another damaged child into this world she went into hospital and returned two weeks later with an eight-inch scar and no womb.

Aunt Caroline took care of my sister and me during that time. Aunt Caroline was a big woman with arms like rolls of carpet and two saddlebags for breasts. To see her move was like watching an overweight heifer master a pair of high heels. The great thing about staying with Aunt Caroline was the ice cream after each meal, and if we helped clean the dishes, if we were quiet and cleaned our rooms, she'd let us listen to the music of Bob Dylan, Jimi Hendrix and The Doors, and watch late night movies where people fell in love, then made love, and then killed each other.

I loved Aunt Caroline, not because she pushed the boundaries of babysitting etiquette, but because she taught us honesty brought out the best in people, and that you should never take yourself too seriously. Above all else, I loved her because she was the mother I so desperately wanted.

When my mother returned from the hospital, everything changed.

Anne Marie had turned fourteen by then. Her fascination towards the opposite sex demanded copious amounts of eyeliner and time away from our fucked up little dynamic. In her absence the tending to each of mother's post surgery needs, fetching of drinks, preparing of light meals, and aiding her to walk short distances, fell to me. My mother gave little compassion towards my predicament. When changing her hospital dressing became part of my chores, and I ran upstairs crying, not once did she concede on her demands. She'd call me the worse son in the world and that there must have been a mix up in the baby ward when I was born.

The scar from my mother's hysterectomy ran just above her pubic hairs. Secured with metal staples, and not surgical thread, the clamped skin beneath preserved a pungent reek of what I remember to be similar to cheese. This stink remained on the white gauze that protected the scar from infection, and it was my job to remove this gauze, put it into a plastic bag and dispose of it in the outside bin. While I did this, she would clean the scar with antiseptic wipes, pulling down the waist of her skirt low enough to reveal the scar, but high enough so it did not reveal anything else.

Now, with my ear to a dying man's chest, I am reminded of that smell once more.

'Can you believe people can live in such a shithole?' asks Prudence from the other side of the room.

I shush her because I think Miller's heart has stopped.

Miller is the name of my old English teacher at school. I chose this for Mr Davidson because they share a similar harelip. The original Miller once made me stand in the front of the class and recite passages from Romeo and Juliet. When I mispronounced a word, or stumbled over the grammar, he hit my hand with a wooden ruler.

'Don't shush me,' Prudence says. 'His chest is still moving.'

Prudence is right. With my head resting on Miller's chest, each forced breath leaving his mouth changes my view of the room. Over his paunch, past his beige trousers and above his leather brogues, I see Prudence sat crossed-legged. With each inhale I catch a glimpse of her eyes reading a sheet of lined paper. With every exhale they are hidden again by the toe of Miller's shoes.

'This place should be condemned. It stinks to high heaven of...'

Beat. Prudence searches to find a likeness to the stench filling the room, a reflection which only moments earlier led me to my mother's scar, one I'm quietly confident Prudence will not draw any similar comparison to.

'Neglect,' she says ruffling the sheet of paper between latex covered fingers.

Proximity forces me to endure Prudence's voice. Any

conversation bringing casualness to these proceedings should be welcomed. Death is no picnic, but there is a job to be done here, learning to be had. I press my ear firmly against Miller's chest, one submerged in a swell of rhythmic pulses, all slowly fading with every second.

'Listen to this,' she says, 'I'm scared. The neighbour's kids play their music too loud and it hurts my ears. I'm lonely. I want to hold someone. I'm lost. Tragic isn't it? To be trapped like that?'

Prudence is reading from the note, her intonation flat and as cold as a mortuary table.

'Do I need to hear that?'

Prudence doesn't answer. She wants me to understand Miller's suffering, to add gravity and reason behind our actions. Either this or she enjoys hearing the agony undertaken by the depressed.

The plight of the suicidal has a tendency to temper my own troubles. For all the pain I have undergone since discovering I have a time bomb ticking in my chest, I never once thought about killing myself. More the opposite. But for those I sit beside, waiting and watching for the last glimmer of life to abandon each eye, the prospect of a long life is more depressing than living it. If only we could exchange bodies. I would happily endure the noisy neighbours and the feeling of loss. I wouldn't mind the stench of cheese around me daily. It is my opinion that to have a heart saddened by life is far better than one broken by it.

I close my eyes and stare deeply into the back of each lid. The sound behind Miller's chest reminds me of the recurring motion of a train journey. Every heartbeat becomes a link in the train track drawing both Miller and I closer to his final destination. I picture Miller sat opposite me in the train carriage. He looks happy. The lines that gave age to his face are gone, smoothed out like fresh linen on hotel beds. The dull nutshell colour of his hair shimmers gold like the patchwork fields of barley beyond our window: his harelip, full and equal to any man's.

Won't be long now, Miller says turning to the window.

His face is at ease as it reflects in each tree and grassy verge he will never touch again. I comment on how easy it is to forget such beauty. And he nods, feeding his eyes on those mythical, white monsters chasing each other through the skies.

Then, like an uninvited rainstorm beating heavy on the window, I hear Prudence's voice from beyond.

'I miss being loved. I miss my mother. I miss company.'

I go back to Miller, to each link in the track growing farther apart. Beyond the carriage window, trees, bushes, and thousand little grey stones clinging to each sleeper make slow progress. Miller turns to me, and says, *It must be time?*

Anticipating the intersection of that final link, Miller stands and takes cautious steps to a small door at the opposite end of the carriage. Before reaching it, he turns and waves his right hand to me.

Everything is wonderful, he says.

I open my eyes. Prudence's face is squeezed tight with suspicion.

'What the hell does that mean?' she asks. 'Everything is wonderful?'

I must have been talking aloud.

I lift myself from Miller's chest. The side of my face is itchy from the wool on his jumper.

'He's gone I take it?' she says returning her attention back to the note.

I ask, 'Do you think it hurts?'

'What?'

When I don't answer she looks up from the note and sees me staring at Miller, his hands unnaturally clenched into claws, mouth agape, the empty reflection in his eyes.

'I shouldn't think so,' she replies. 'I guess it depends on how you go. I'm no expert but opening your veins is far more painful than taking an overdose.'

Prudence joins me beside Miller.

'Here,' she says, handing me the note. 'I'm sure if there is any pain in death, it would be marginal to what he had to deal with while alive.'

The note in my hand is barely legible. Most of the words look more like hieroglyphics drawn by a small child. Those not tapering off awkwardly into a series of arcs are smudged. On Miller's claw-like hand, blue ink smears his little finger.

While Miller wrote what would become his final declaration, I was waiting in his garden, hunched behind a thick leylandii. Prudence felt that due to my eye it would be best if I wait there until Miller finished his tea. This is why today there is no back history to develop, no new alias to remember, because by the time

I entered his home, Miller was already dying. Prudence administered a lethal antidepressant overdose and put into operation a plan that would help pacify any suspicion the local police department might have regarding our unconventional therapy sessions.

This is what happens: over tea and biscuits, Prudence explains to the patient/victim how the government has introduced a new scheme for patients dealing with depression. Those with repeat prescriptions for dispositional drugs like Prozac, Paxil, Zoloft and Lithium, will need quarterly assessments on their current state of mind to help research and fund the progressive use of such drugs in the future. In conjunction with this, pharmacists, and their staff, will have to manage various recommended guidance techniques to help each patient overcome any difficulties they may have should the drugs not be working effectively. One of these is a technique called, Cognitive Restructuring, a term Prudence overheard in a conversation between two physicians at the hospital. She explains to the victim that the underlying principle lay heavily in patient participation. When feeling either saddened or apprehensive, the patient/victim will be asked to write down any negative thoughts on a piece of paper to help them overcome any worries they may be harbouring. The theory being that once the patient/victim can see each negative thought in front of them, it is easier to understand it is only their own mind creating those anxieties and worries, thus helping them to manage and resolve any issues.

I place the note that holds Miller's pain within his hand, and though inside my stomach is pulled tight with twine, and my conscience jagged as gator skin, Prudence's idea to get the victims to write their own suicide note appeases my troubled heart.

In my mind, a warm voice whispers the words: Everything is wonderful.

CHAPTER 11

Two metal studs poke out of the taxi driver's neck, dull and lifeless like Manta Ray eyes. I ask Prudence why anyone would go through such pain and she triggers the little black button on her disposable camera, one that brings with it an atomic blast of white light.

'Would you mind if I take your picture?' she asks the taxi driver. He twists his huge neck around to face her, small folds of skin forming along his nape, creating bigger folds that run up to his big cauliflower ear where more studs reside. I glance quickly at this man, trying not to make excessive eye contact. He's a beast. A mountain. A totem of flesh and bone punctured by metal. Upon his arm Death's bony carcass fucks an archangel from behind. Death's eyes are the colour of pumpkins. A serpent's trunk, thick and meaty, trails out from between where the angel's vagina should be, if angels had vaginas.

'The angel looks familiar,' Prudence says, noticing the tattoo.

The brute speaks.

'Jenna Jameson,' he says with a tone that shakes my bones.

'The porn actress?' Prudence asks.

He replies, 'You know her work?'

Prudence smiles and takes a picture of the tattoo. I haven't watched porn for a long time. There is a fear that my heart may fail if I do. No man wants to be found by paramedics, frozen in time, hand firmly clamped around their penis. To retain some dignity, even in death, I have taken a vow of celibacy. But Prudence puts that to test daily. She is my Mary Magdalene. My Cleopatra. My serpent.

The cabby turns his arm over so the underside is facing Prudence's camera. Inked in black, and running its full length, are the words: Ye shall not make any cuttings in your flesh for the dead, nor print any marks upon you: I am the LORD. Leviticus 19:28

Another atomic blast fills the cab. I blink and the same words are projected on the back of his chair in negative.

'You should get one of those,' Prudence says to me, referring to the tattoo.

I shake my head.

Four minutes into the journey and Prudence leans over me to draw a big heart on the steamed up window. In the heart she writes my name. She then takes a picture of it.

'The halo effect,' I say.

'What?' she asks.

'Light from the flash will reflect off the window creating a halo effect. Sometimes it's referred to as light at the end of the tunnel. Where I work, there is an advice label for this.'

Prudence gives me a peculiar look.

'You mean where you *used* to work?' she asks.

I tell her that's what I meant.

Prudence taking pictures of steamed up windows and taxi driver's body art is her way of coping.

Yesterday she told me about an old photo album she has. The photo album contains pictures of nobody but Prudence. Not one of the pictures shows her smiling. Every day at work I see families with their arms linked, teeth exposed, all of them looking happy. Prudence hasn't got one solitary picture where her teeth are revealed. She told me it didn't bother her, and that she doesn't look at herself in them anymore. Prudence concentrates on the little things that make up the rest of the image instead, like the dress she wore, or the shoes, the wallpaper, her posters. The bits and pieces of her life that held no real consequence at the time now mean more to Prudence than seeing herself growing up.

"Bits and pieces," she said to me. "The little things that make the difference."

I can't imagine Prudence being young, vulnerable and dependent on someone else. She doesn't talk about her past, but something terrible happened when she was young. She won't tell me what, and frankly, I don't really want to know. I like not knowing. I would hate to know everything about a person because then there would be nothing more you could know. Once you know everything, a relationship becomes dull and repetitive. But the little I hear about her childhood saddens me greatly.

Prudence rolls the window down and points the camera at a cyclist who has pulled up beside the taxi. She says my face is burnt into her mind forever, which is why she never needs to see a photograph of it. What she wants to remember now are the little things that make the difference, like the way I stack my CD collection, the way I fold towels, the books I read, my shoes, and the holes in my jumpers. What she needs to be reminded of today is the taxi journey to my mother's house.

CHAPTER 12

We're met at the door by a cloud of grey smoke that smells like cut grass and basil. The noise of a thousand rusty saws cutting through sheet metal can be heard from a room somewhere within the house. A kid, no more than twenty-years of age, appears shielding his eyes from the sunlight.

'Fuck, dude,' he says, the words struggling to leave his mouth.

Each nail on the kid's hand is as black as his T-shirt. Face is as pale as suffocated skin under a band aid. Hair long and the colour of piss stains on white cotton. All at once a chill runs over me at the possibility that this kid, this little stoner, could be my mother's new fuck buddy.

'Is Verity in?' I ask.

The shutter opens on Prudence's camera. Click!

He shouts to someone in the house to turn down the buzz saw noise before giving me the international sign to repeat the question by cupping his hand behind his ear. When I do, his forehead and eyes pull together collectively making him look Japanese.

'You Five-O?!' he shouts.

I shake my head and tell him, 'I'm Verity's son.'

'You're very what?!'

Turning to face the hall again, he shouts, 'Turn the shit down!'

A few seconds later the noise from behind him stops. He turns back to Prudence and me and barely breaks a smile.

'What now?' he asks.

A voice calls out. With sunken, dark eyes and rutted brow, I see her break through the cloud of dope smoke like a ghoul. With her hand resting on the stoner's shoulder, she says, 'He said, he's my son.'

Verity guides us through varying cobwebs of smoke to our old kitchen. The mouse squeak of her thighs as they rub together in a pair of ridiculously tight leather pants accompanies our steps. Through her vest, which looks tailored from a fisherman's net, I see a black bra strap cutting into white flesh.

'For her age, your mother has a great arse,' Prudence whispers.

This is a bad idea. Actually, this is Prudence's idea.

She convinced me a couple of days ago that it is never good for a person to carry over too much resentment towards another person into the next life. Prudence believes my spirit might never rest without atonement. I tried convincing her no amount of compassion, or empathy, shown my mother would change the fact she is a ten-carat cunt, but Prudence insisted I try. I secretly believe my spirit's sanity is only partly the reason for our visit today. Prudence's sheer doggedness towards reconciliation could be a guise, one that allows Prudence to see firsthand if my mother is as terrible as I have made her out to be. There is little she accepts without true understanding. This is the reason I believe in her theories about death, and why I have engaged so willingly in the act of murder. To attempt to instruct another on such a delicate and contentious subject without fully understanding it would be akin to a blind man teaching a child to drive a car.

The kitchen hasn't changed. Given it's only been five months since I was last here I expected evidence of disrepair, neglect manifesting into mould running the full length of each teak work surface, possibly a loose handle on a cupboard needing tightening. I have to admit, with the place looking so organised and well-kept, I'm disappointed. The only noticeable change is in Verity. Her hair, which has always been a tired and a dull blonde, similar to Miller's, is now the same shade of black found in comic strip superheroes. With the sun pouring in from the window, it shimmers in varying shades of blue, something that matches perfectly with the thick mascara circling each eye.

'Who's the kid?' I ask nodding my head towards the door.

Verity pulls out a cigarette, lights it, and offers the pack to us. We both decline. This is her way of regaining authority in our estranged little fucked up dynamic. The longer I wait for an answer the more in control she feels.

Blowing smoke in my face she says, 'You mean, Taupe.'

'Like the colour?'

'Sure, like the colour,' she says taking another drag.

'You screwing him?' I ask.

Verity smiles and turns to Prudence.

Holding out her hand she says, 'You'll have to forgive my son. His manners are as elusive as he is these days.'

Prudence introduces herself and I oversee formal introductions with a keen eye.

'Are you my son's fuck buddy?' she asks.

Now it's time for Prudence to smile. They both look to me.

I tell Verity, 'Prudence is my friend.'

She exhales a stream of smoke towards the brown cork ceiling.

'Girl...friend?'

This is the first time anyone has ever asked this question. I'm unsure how to respond. It's a risk but I nod my head. Then I look to Prudence. She holds no expression to say I was right or wrong.

'In answer to your question, I'm screwing his manager,' says Verity turning to me. 'Taupe is in his band. I let them use my basement.'

I ask if that's a euphemism but Verity doesn't acknowledge me.

'Was that what we could hear playing when we arrived?' Prudence asks sounding more enthusiastic than needed.

Verity flicks the ash off her cigarette and nods her head.

'You like thrash metal?' she asks Prudence.

'Thrash? No, not really. It sounded interesting, though.'

Verity opens a drawer next to her and pulls out a yellow flyer with big thick writing on.

Handing it to Prudence, she says, 'The band's called, Matricide. They're playing tomorrow night at a place in the city called, Doom. Use this and you'll get in for free. You really need to see them live.'

Prudence ponders over the flyer like she's picking sushi.

I ask Verity where they got their name. I'm not interested but I want the conversational pendulum to swing both ways. Besides, I know how manipulative Verity can be. If she gets Prudence on her side then it will be much harder for me to come out of this the better person.

After a long, hard drag on her cigarette, Verity replies with, 'It's the act of killing your mother.' She lets out another stream of smoke above our heads and adds, 'They all have issues.'

'Maybe I should join,' I tell her, and Prudence slaps my arm.

'That's okay, honey, I had that one coming,' says Verity. 'So is that why you've come back, to tell me I'm a terrible mother?'

'Maybe I should give you both some time alone,' says Prudence folding the flyer into her back pocket.

Verity walks over to the sink and runs her cigarette under the tap.

'I don't think that's necessary, hon,' she says.

Verity turns and walks to me. Stopping inches from my face, so close I smell the burnt treacle smell of smoke on her breath, she says, 'You don't mind do you?'

For a second I'm unsure what she means. Then she points to the bin behind me.

I shrug my shoulders and move a little to one side; just enough so Verity can slip the toe of her shoe between my legs to activate the pedal that lifts the bin's lid. She moves forward, her body twisting around mine like grape vines suffocating the trunk of a decaying tree. Her mouth, a few centimetres away from my ear, beats a faint wheeze magnified for me and no one else. I play the noise back in my head and it reminds me of the sound Ilse's made before she died, a moment that seems so very far away now. As quickly as she arrived, Verity is back in front of the window looking at me, face self-satisfied with how the scene played out.

'Why is it not necessary?' Prudence asks Verity.

'I don't think my son would have brought you here today if you didn't know everything that's happened between us. Isn't that right?'

I give Prudence a sideways glance and note her face is cast in grey. I turn to Verity, noting the two corners of her mouth rising. Creases gather either side like theatre curtains parting to reveal some sinister play.

'What does she mean?' Prudence asks me.

Before I have chance to reply, Verity says, 'I'm sure my son has made it clear how terrible a mother I've been. How I lied about his daddy, and the poor unfortunate situation he's now in because of it. I'm quite sure he would tell you everything. Am I right, Jack?'

I'm a block of stone frozen in a glacier.

'You must know about me,' Verity says, 'what I've done to him over the years?'

The world around Verity melts away: the teak cupboards, the window, and the sky beyond, all of it a jumble of twisted colour melting together into one big lump of shit. Looking at my mother's face, all I see is the tip of her tongue rubbing itself against the bottom row of teeth.

'There's no need for you to go and be leaving the room, Prudence. There are no secrets here. Or is there?' Verity asks me. 'Prudence does know everything, right?'

Hands lock at the thumb. The shape they've made is the same when attempting a shadow puppet of a bird. Before I know it the bird has flown to Verity's throat, its wings wrapped tight. I call her a witch and a bitch! Prudence's screams perforate the smoke hovering above us. Verity's eyes are bulging, each one appearing rounder and more defined than they should. Knuckles now white as the bone beneath. Spittle lands in pools upon her cheek and brow. I reaffirm my grip around her neck, a neck dry as rotten wood, probably just as weak and fragile too. The bird's wingspan shortens as I feel Prudence's hands pulling on my shoulders. Verity begins making rapid, little breaths.

'Your heart!' Prudence cries.

I feel a sharp pain across my back. Knees crack against the linoleum. Lungs shrivel like two plastic bags held near an open fire. For at least ten seconds I am robbed of breath. My hands stretch out in front of me, almost touching Verity's black-leather high heels. The ice cube cracking sound in my chest comes with the first new breath. The second makes me light-headed. Before I take pleasure in the third, my ribs take the full force of a shoe. Not Verity's shoe. They're still close to my fingers, or were, because I'm now in the foetal position gasping for air. Prudence's face in front of mine, tears welling, nose shiny with snot.

'Try that again and I'll go all fucking Bruce Lee on you, dude.'

Taupe.

'Oh baby... You okay?' Prudence asks.

Struggling for breath stops me from having to provide a coherent answer. Prudence stands up and I hear her arguing with Taupe. I hear her screaming at him that there was no need to hit me with a rolling pin. In the background, my mother is coughing. Minutes fall around me like raindrops, soaking me in spells of repose. I figure it would take a downpour to lessen my pain and a flood to stop the sound of Prudence and Taupe screaming at each other. Eventually the gap between each of their retorts widens, and with all my being, I wish the pain in my back and sides would show me the same courtesy. When I finally muster enough strength to pull myself to my feet, only Prudence is in the room.

'A taxi is on its way,' she says. 'We need to get you looked at. That idiot could have broken something.'

I tell her there's no need.

'There's every need, Jack,' she says. 'You could die through internal bleeding.'

'I'm dying anyhow,' I say.

'Not like this.'

'Then how?' I ask under the weight of heavy breaths.

'I don't know. Just not this way.'

'A shift of heart,' I say.

'What?'

Exploring heart problems has led me to stumble upon many things. The same books I use to memorise the affects of drug overdoses also share space with other periodicals and publications relating to health concerns. One passage I read described a sudden shift of heart. It seemed a strange term to use, a shift of heart, especially in a medical reference book. If anything, the term is better suited for a novel, like when someone's emotions change favourably towards someone else, or like now, when all my good intentions of reconciliation change course because of my bitch-whore mother and her snide comments. But the term used in the medical book held no similarity or relation to emotion. What I remember about the paragraph is hazy, but it seems a well-aimed and forcefully administered blow is the ideal tool to help snap a rib and puncture a lung. If untreated, the lung will collapse causing a shift of heart, trachea and oesophagus. This change causes the compression of the opposite lung, affecting the flow of blood returning to the heart. So Prudence is right; I could die as the result of my injuries. And maybe she's right too that it's not my time yet. Maybe there is something I need to do, destiny or some other shit. All of this sounds fucking absurd in my head, a lot of cosmic nonsense, but with the pain in my sides, and the threat of dying right here in Verity's kitchen, I decide time spent with Prudence understanding death is a much better alternative than experiencing it tonight.

I'm snapped back into the room by the beat of Verity's shoes striking the linoleum.

'Taupe has gone,' she says rubbing her neck, throat scratchy. 'I said I'd be safe as long as Prudence was around. He's a good kid really.'

'He's a psycho,' Prudence says putting her arm across my shoulder.

I'm half expecting Verity to say the very same about me, but instead she bites down on her bottom lip while hooking her fringe behind her ear.

'I've made up your spare room. You should both stay tonight. We need to iron a few things out.'

The pain in my back and side demands too much attention from me. Even the thought of responding to such an absurd idea seems to aggravate it.

'We have a taxi coming,' says Prudence, saving me the effort.

'We can use it to go to the hospital,' suggests Verity. 'And then we can come back and I'll cook us all something to eat.'

Silence.

Prudence turns to me waiting for an answer. I look to Verity who's waiting for an answer too. Maybe it's the dull, incessant throb radiating through my bones, or hearing Verity's voice straining from my grip, whatever it is, I find myself nodding in agreement to Verity's request.

Another shift of heart.

#

A hospital waiting room where seconds stretched out before me like acres of marshland, with cold fingers pressing hard on the tender parts of my body, of inelegance and partial nudity required when receiving an x-ray, and the verdict; hairline fracture to my left rib and bruised spine. When Prudence and Verity walked me out of Willow Bank A&E it was dark. But I would, without a second thought, relive every respite in conversation, every awkward breath and forced pleasantry exchanged between Verity and Prudence a thousand times over if it meant not being here at this dinner table with Harry.

'I once fractured my coccyx,' Harry says.

Harry is Matricide's manager. He's also my mother's new fuck buddy. Roll back twenty years and Harry would have been, Uncle Harry. Verity hasn't mentioned anything about what happened earlier. She's even gone so far as to change her vest for a roll neck sweater to hide my finger marks. The emotional guilt trip to get

Prudence and me to return back to her home was an expedition in manipulation. Rubbing her neck, clearing her throat every five seconds, that was only half of it. She did everything to make me feel like shit for trying to strangle her. But that wasn't the reason Prudence and I came. The real reason was to save any further complications. Who knows what a woman like Verity would do. To act callous towards her now might make her do likewise, and the last thing both Prudence and I need is a visit from the police chasing up claims of assault. It was best to go with the flow, finish the meal as quickly as possible and get the fuck out of here.

Tapping his fork on a honey-coloured tombstone jutting from his top gum, Harry says, 'Fractured it on account of this sweet tooth.'

Harry throws a big old smile at Prudence and my arse cheeks clench.

'Maybe this isn't the best conversation for the dinner table, honey,' Verity says.

Harry turns to Prudence and says, 'You're okay with it, right, sweetheart?'

'Not every Prudence is a prude,' she replies, smiling.

Harry undresses her with his eyes for as moment before turning to me.

'And you?' he asks.

I'm still reeling from the way Prudence smiled at Harry.

'And me what?' I ask.

'You a prude?'

I don't say anything.

Verity interjects, 'Everything okay, Jack?'

Her face is warped into a mask of pained unease. I like it.

'I'm dandy,' I say to Harry.

He nods slowly. The shit-eating grin on his face makes me want to jump over the table and stick my fork in his eye, but I keep telling myself this will be over soon and Prudence and I can go back to the norm of killing manic depressives and lonely hearts.

Harry makes a sound like a punctured tyre and turns his attention back to Prudence and Verity.

'So I was working nights at a chocolate factory. This was way before I got into the managing game. God, it must have been, I don't know, fifteen years back. I was the security guard there. It wasn't a great job. I mean, security work isn't. But it did allow me to graze the company's stock.'

I know somewhere in the country someone is happy. At this exact moment in time they're smiling in front of a camera, and not one of those phony smiles you see on celebrities, but a real smile that causes contractions of the orbicularis oculi muscles around the eyes. If the skin around the eyes is loose, they're faking. I've seen so many during my time as a Grader I can separate whose genuinely happy from those who are not by their eyes alone. If you were to look at my eyes right now, the skin around them would be loose.

'So there was some promotion on a new caramel bar. What was the name of it? Caravel? Carma —'

'I don't think it matters, honey,' Verity says, the desperation in her voice like birdsong to me.

'Well, whatever it was called, there were boxes of them hanging around the offices, half open. You used to get freebies all the time, chocolate bars, candy sticks, fizzy drinks, so I figured I'd tried one. I'll tell you this, Prudence; by the time my shift ended I'd gotten through twenty-five bars! Can you believe that? My tummy was bigger than the belly of a starving Rwandan kid.'

Harry sticks out his stomach and pats it.

The way Harry tells the story, you know over the fifteen years since eating that first bar he's added twice the amount consumed.

I look over to Verity. She's staring right at me. Eyes two empty graves dug out of snow. I feel the chill of winter run across my aching body.

'Thing was,' says Harry, 'after a few days all that caramel hardened in my colon. I was blocked tighter than a nun's chuff.'

I grab hold of Prudence's hand and begin stroking it.

'I couldn't shit for love nor money,' says Harry. 'Every time I tried I was in agony. Now, I'm not one for doctors. Verity knows. I've only ever been twice that I can remember. So the last thing I wanted to do was bend over in front of one and have him stick his finger up my hole.'

Harry thrusts his index finger through a tight little O shape he's made with his opposite fist.

I yawn.

'So I went into the kitchen, boiled up some hot water in a pan and popped in two teaspoons.'

Unable to stomach another word, I say, 'For once I'm in agreement with my mother; homemade rectal surgery isn't suitable for the dinner table, Harry.'

'Your son should learn some manners, Verity,' Harry says.

'He doesn't mean anything by it, Harry,' Verity says.

'That right?' he asks me.

'Sure,' I tell him, dragging out the word like a piece of chewing gum from my lips.

'You know, Verity mentioned that about you. You like to speak your mind,' he says.

I look over to Verity whose picking up a loose shrimp from her plate. I watch as the small section of its dismembered torso rests momentarily on her bottom lip, her long painted fingernails twirling it over and over.

Harry says, 'She said it's got you in trouble before.'

'If that were true,' I say to Harry, 'I'd probably have said much more than I have already.'

'Cut the attitude, eh kid? You ain't no Chuck Norris.'

'Who?'

'Maybe we should get going,' says Prudence. 'It's been a long day and I'm quite sure we all need the rest.'

Turning to me, Harry asks, 'What did you say was wrong with you again?'

'Tripped over several cans of paint,' I say.

Verity bites down hard on the shrimp before asking, 'I thought you both were going to stay over? I made the bed especially.'

Prudence shakes her head. 'I have work, no change of clothes and...' There's a slight pause before she says to me, 'You have things to do. Don't you, Jack?'

'I have some clothes I'm sure would fit you, Prudence.' Turning to me, Verity asks, 'Prudence and I are about a similar size, right?'

I fill my mouth with wine. I'm not supposed to be drinking. The doctor said I should stay off alcohol while taking the Voltarol he subscribed for my pain, but the thought of seeing Prudence dressed up like some cheap hooker is all too much.

'Harry keeps a few spare T-shirts and things here, too,' she says.

I look at Harry's attire: a black Led Zeppelin T-shirt with black leather waistcoat.

I take another swig of wine.

'Let them be,' says Harry. 'If they don't want to stay, don't force'em.'

'It's probably for the best,' says Prudence. 'Besides, I can't stand wearing the same underwear two days in a row.'

Verity replies, 'Borrow some of mine, if you like?'

Six hours in hospital are short-lived daydreams compared to this.

'Prudence is right,' I say. 'We need to get going.'

'But you never asked about Anne Marie.'

Begrudgingly I indulge her, 'How is she?'

'She's fine, but —'

'Good.'

Beat.

'What about the band?' she asks Prudence.

'Let'em go, Verity. He told you he'll be back. You can both catch up properly then.'

I suggest to Prudence we call a taxi and wait outside.

The sound of rain pelting the umbrella reminds me of bacon frying. The cold air makes visible every breath I take. Steam rises and fades from my nose, diminishing as quickly as it appears, similar to the rain bouncing off the road in front of us, each drop a little white crown worn by a water king. Since leaving Verity and Harry, Prudence hasn't said one word to me. I look to her and note thick fog pouring from each of her nostrils, fierce and incessant like that of an angry bull. I make small talk, commenting on the weather, but it doesn't help. Prudence is pissed.

Two small headlights, faint and abandoned in a blizzard of rain, push their way towards us through the unfurling blackness of the road. The pace and the sound of the engine suggest it's the taxi. I wave my hands in the air. It starts to hurt my back so I stop. I block the rain from my eyes and look ahead; the car's headlamps are motionless, hovering like two cat's eyes on a country road. I arrive at the conclusion it's not the taxi but another car parking outside a nearby house. I'm about to tell Prudence to give the taxi firm another ring on her mobile when the headlamps begin growing in size. I was wrong. It is the taxi. It must have been lost and nothing more.

I look to Prudence and she stares ahead, lost in the darkness too.

CHAPTER 13

Under the double strip fluorescent lights, Desmond's skin looks the colour of damp bricks. His hair is lighter, a mousy brown lightened by the sun. He's put on a few pounds too, around his waist and a little on his face, but not too much, just enough to make him look healthier. He is an opposite of disproportional measure to me. Every moment spent in his company makes me more aware of my drop in weight, the bags hanging from each eye, the paleness of my skin, the weight of six feet of earth bearing down on my shoulders.

'Mick tells me you want a chat?' says Desmond.

I shift my weight, smile. Skin around the eyes relaxed.

'You want to sit?' he asks.

I tell him no. 'I'm fine standing,' I say.

Outside his office, the hum of machinery, the clatter of pistons, the sound of an FLT reversing, they all ground me in reality.

What am I even doing here? This need to explain myself, the need to be forgiven, it makes no logical sense. In less than a month I will be dead, and this conversation will mean nothing to me, or Desmond. Yet since promising Prudence I would quit my job, I have felt an obligation to explain to him why it is I'm handing in my resignation. It is the right thing to do. Aunt Caroline would approve. If someone offers you their time and patience, it is good manners to give them the same in return.

I look over his shoulder, through his window and onto the work floor.

If you spend enough time in one particular place, you become accustomed to how it functions. You know what to expect. Like the A&E department at the hospital; different people come in with different ailments and injuries, but the one constant is the pain and the fear they carry. Everyone who enters that place is scared, hurting, and regardless of who accompanies them, husband, wife, lover, father or mother, they're alone, because no one else in that whole place understands what they're going through at that exact moment. You get used to this. You expect it.

Desmond calls out my name and says, 'If there is something you want to talk about then sooner would be better.'

If I tender my resignation at Colour Inc, every day will be different. Nothing will be constant. Here people sit at their desks and they work until the whistle blows. They don't talk. They don't moan. Save for taking a piss and eating their dinner, they remain constant in their undertaking: film is developed, film is processed, photographs are produced, and photographs are dispatched. It's a simple chain of events that never changes, regardless of weather, sickness or death. This job, with its many spools of happy memories, and the A&E department at the hospital with its pain and suffering, they are the only dependable things in my life. And however sad that may sound, knowing there is something out there that will not change regardless of intervention makes me forget how fragile my life is. They provide me with comfort. The part Prudence plays in all this is – she makes me want to live for the day when I don't need the constant and stability.

'No,' I say. 'There's nothing pressing I need to discuss. I just wanted to ask about your holiday; where was it again? Bora Bora, how wonderful. I'm thinking of going. Would you recommend your resort? Really? How wonderful. Well, I won't take up any more of your time, considering you probably have quite a lot to catch up on. Thank you again, Desmond.'

Less than five minutes later I push up the lever on the grading table and see photographs of Koi Carp, an interracial wedding, a beach holiday. Around me, people move like ice skaters. Nobody pays attention to anyone else. They glide past me with papers in their hands, spools of film, cardboard wallets. Here, nothing changes. Everything is constant.

CHAPTER 14

Red carnations and gypsy breath and stems bent by strong winds. I take these out of the pots, trim them with my fingers, and place them back. It's a nice bouquet, simple. The colours work well against the black granite of my father's gravestone. I read the card attached, shrink-wrapped: Happy Birthday Daddy, love Anne Marie.

Verity hasn't told her yet, but Anne Marie has every right to know this is not our father's birthday, or his final resting place. She needs to know if only to prepare herself should she bring a son into the world. If only to prepare herself that she will never see him live beyond thirty years.

Taking a handkerchief from my pocket, I wipe down the epitaph. Clouds gather over me, huddling and conspiring in mockery, like they know the grave is empty and I'm a fool for tending to it. I hate those clouds. Anger builds in me and the need to purge my frustration is great. I look over to the rectory and think about the priest. He's old and today is a very cold day. I remember what he said about the kitchen and how it is the warmest room in the rectory. I picture him there in moccasins, reading Genesis or looking curiously into cupboards. In addition to wanting to make sure he is warm and well, it would be good for me to speak to him about Prudence and the trouble we've been having since our meal with Verity. He can be my counsel and the balm to soothe my irritability.

The rectory sits in its own grounds. Winter trees that remind me of burnt corpses surround its four walls. I knock on the heavy wooden door and wait. No answer. I press my ear against the door, listening for the shuffling of feet, but all I hear is the wind singing its ballad of derision toward me. I knock again, louder this time. It hurts my knuckles. He must be in the church doing whatever it is priests do during the day.

The church is poorly lit, the furnishings a dark brown reminding me of home. Small candles light up pictures of Jesus' crucifixion and pre-Raphaelite images of Mary at his blood-soaked feet. Around her head shines an arc of pure gold. Mary was a good mother. Not like Verity. Would she cry at my feet if men speared my sides? Would she soak up my blood with rags? Would she even be there to watch me die, her only son, sacrificing myself for the whole of mankind? Like fuck she would.

I take a seat on the back pew. With head bowed it occurs to me I have no idea what it is you're supposed to do in a church. The believers come to pray, but I have never been a praying man. God has enough to deal with without me bending His ear. I decide to look instead at the walls, the stain glass windows, altar and sacrament table. Timber struts draped either side of the domed ceiling remind me of thick, black gills. The line of red carpet pouring from the sacrament table reminds me of a tongue. Realising this makes me laugh, only a little at first, but it soon gathers momentum. The more I think about all those people brought here by the consequences of their sins, to spend time in this great whale waiting for God to grant them a pardon so they can be spat out into the world again, like that trickster Jonah, makes me double over with laughter. In every dark recess and dusty corner of the church my laughter collects. When it finds its way back to me, every cackle and snigger sounds baleful and unfamiliar. I hold my mouth and feel tears running down my fingers. Shoulders shake violently. My mind projects upon its silver screen awful images: mutilation, conjoined twins, the effects of Agent Orange; anything to help calm each spasm. I see Christ's painful trial and torturous suffering on every limestone wall and stained glass window: blood-stained hands punctured by nails, brow bloodied and scarred with each of man's sins, His feeble body chosen to suffer a life of agony and persecution by His own father. And here I am, laughing like a madman.

From behind me comes a raspy cough. Like two accordions duelling out a merry song for drunks, my lungs pull tight then release, pull tight and release, and as the person draws near, I hold both hands to my mouth, bending over as if praying. As their shadow brushes mine, I look up and see an old lady dressed in a long, black coat. Grabbing the side of a pew in front, she kneels slightly and crosses her chest before taking a seat. I leave the pew and make a fast dash towards the door where the mouth of this great whale awaits. Outside the cold October breeze strokes my face and daylight presses hard on each eye. I return to the rectory.

I knock again but there is still no reply.

'You won't find the priest in there,' says a voice.

I turn to see the same old woman from the church, a brown shawl wrapped tightly around her face so each cheek appears the same shade as a ripe plum.

'Where is he?' I ask.

'Last I heard he'd taken ill a couple of days back.'

I move towards her.

'I could do with speaking with him. Do you know where he's gone?'

The old woman looks at me with unease. She either thinks I'm mad, dangerous, or both. To reassure her I am neither, I tell her I'm an old friend of the family, an estranged nephew wishing to speak to his uncle, the priest.

'I've had a run of bad luck recently,' I add. 'My father, a proud man, believes I should reconcile my problems alone. But I've tried and failed. So here I am, wishing to be heard by the one person who has the patience and the words to get me through this difficult time.'

Save for the wind, there is nothing between the old woman and me but silence.

I break the deadlock by asking her if there's anything she knows, anything to help me track down my uncle.

'Couldn't you ring round and find out where your uncle is?' she asks. 'I'm quite sure someone in your family would know.'

She's right, a fundamental flaw in my story. Prudence would have concocted a much more plausible story standing on her head.

'Of course.' I say. 'I wasn't thinking straight. My mind is all over the place because of all the stress I've been under. I'll go and see my other aunt, the priest's sister. I'm sure she knows where I can find my uncle. Thank you.'

'I thought Father Branigan was an only child? He's mentioned it a few times in his sermons.'

'He is,' I say quickly. 'I meant his sister-in-law, through marriage you understand? It's my mother's sister I will approach about the location of my uncle.'

Every part of her face shifts south. She's not at all convinced of my story. I don't blame her.

'I best be heading back,' she says. 'If I see Father Branigan, I'll be sure to pass it on you've been asking for him. What was your name again?'

I tell her, 'Jonah.'

'Like the whale?'

'Like the whale,' I say.

As I watch her walk over the gravestones, past the angel statue and towards the main gate, thoughts go back to the priest and if his illness is serious, where he might be, how long he will be gone, and when I can visit him again. He's the only person in the world right now I believe would understand my reasons for trying to choke my mother. And if I was to explain how weird Prudence was after we left my mother's house, I'm sure he would know why. He may want more details before drawing a solid conclusion, so I'd tell him how I tried talking it out with Prudence when we got back to my flat, but she just clammed up, putting her mood down to her period. But I know Prudence witnessed that oddity between Verity and I. She saw Verity the way I saw her, not so much a mother, but something else, something more sinister. But Prudence won't talk about it with me. And that's all I need to do right now; talk. I wish the priest was here. He'd listen to me and maybe help me understand it all too. But he's not. He's ill and I am left forsaken.

CHAPTER 15

The Egyptians believed the heart represented the centre of a person's personality, the very seat of the soul. During mummification, the heart became the only organ the embalmers didn't move entirely from the body.

I look over to Prudence and she's already looking through the lens of her camera at a brown mallard slicing through the mercury-coloured lake in front of us. I hear the shutter open and realise that mallard will forever be the symbol of this conversation.

Breaking apart small pieces of bread, I tell Prudence, 'The heart became a passport to the next life. Before admittance was given, the heart had to be presented to the correct authorities.'

I throw the bread and eight ducks appear from behind a green fern.

'In the Book of the Dead,' I say, 'it told how the heart would be weighed on a scale against the feather of Ma'at, an ostrich feather taken from the goddess of physical and moral law. If the heart is as light as the feather, the deceased would be granted eternal life with the Egyptian god Osiris. If it were heavier, Ammut, a creature with the head of a crocodile, the body of a lion and the backside of a hippopotamus, would feast greedily on their soul. According to the Egyptians, a heart so light must be pure, but a heart so heavy must be weighed down with sin and evil.'

I tell Prudence how my mother's heart would break that scale in fucking two.

'I need to know what happened, Jack. What did she do to you?'

It's been a week since the dinner with Verity. Prudence has spent most of that time avoiding me. I've attended the A&E every morning as usual. When I saw her enter the building, I'd follow her to the prescriptions department, and like some fawning teenage fool, ask why she hadn't returned any of my calls. The same reply came my way: she'd been too busy.

Prudence didn't even make eye contact.

Yesterday, I told her that I will do whatever it takes to return things back to normal. She looked at me and said all she wanted was the truth.

Now, sat on the embankment to a small boating lake close to the hospital, I say, 'That's the one thing I can't tell you.'

'You can't or you won't?'

'It's more that I don't know if I can.'

Prudence puts her camera in a plastic bag and turns to face me. I am wretched beyond measure at the barrenness of each eye, the desolation of their stare. No part of Prudence is familiar to me at all now. My clandestine has robbed her of intimacy, erased all feelings.

She tells me, 'I don't know if I can trust you anymore.'

I wish to hold her, to feel the smoothness of her cheekbone against my finger. If I had only five beats in my heart remaining, I would gladly hand each over to see Prudence look upon me with the understanding of a friend, or the compassion of a lover. To surrender my life would not be enough for Prudence. Only the truth about Verity and I will return her to me. My fear is at what cost.

I throw another chunk of bread and two ducks both fight for it.

'I want us to trust each other again,' I say.

'Then tell me.'

So I do.

My mother's bed was a spire four-poster that smelt of a person's breath after they'd missed two main meals. Its timber was forever grouchy and irritable, complaining incessantly whenever one of my uncles visited. Verity never stayed downstairs to save her children this indignity. Most nights her giggling, which followed the deep disjointed rumble of a man's voice, would awaken me and I would be subjected to the discomfort of hearing their groans bleeding through my bedroom wall. To a child, night threw a cloak over empty spaces and gave form to things that were not there. Its muted voice and muggy breath transformed harmless sounds into morbid clamour, so the moans and heavy breath from your mother became a ghoul caught between worlds. The heavy beat of a man's breath became the Devil. For hours after the noise of my mother and her new lover had dissipated, I remained stock-still, frozen with fear. Shadows swanked around the bedroom, painting each wall a deep black that turned shallow corners into infinite caverns. As cars passed beneath my window, headlamps pierced the wooden blinds projecting giant piano keys across a charcoal-grey ceiling. Within a few hours, a room as small as my bedroom, become immeasurable.

Hearing the front door slam shut and a man's footsteps pressing heavily into the gravel path beyond my window allowed my joints to finally loosen, freeing me to grab my pillow, sneak into my mother's room on all fours, and crawl under her bed. To be close to her without being chastised or struck for being insolent and confrontational, two things I am sure most children were from time to time, was a curiosity. Being beneath her bed, listening to her breathing, kindled within me an informal bond. I would move shoeboxes, and her collection of Linda Ronstadt LPs, to make space for my tired little body. The metrical beat of her breath was a chloroform rag putting me into a deep slumber that never broke until the morning. Before she awoke, I would sneak back into my room, get into bed and rest there until I was called for breakfast.

Roll back two years before her hysterectomy: I'm lay under her bed when a distant but fervent noise pulled me from the Sandman's hands. Whimpering. Whining. The mattress groaned as her weight shifted across it. I lay there listening to the randomness of her mind, the heavy breath that carried from her mouth obscure and undeveloped words. The noises above me resembled that of a person lost to the delirium of a fever. I was worried for her, but I knew if I appeared from under the bed she would never allow me back in. So I waited until Verity's whimpering, and the squeak of mattress, allowed me the opportunity to roll out quietly without being heard. I'll never forget the colour of that room in those early hours. Everything with life looked lifeless, and everything with beauty turned ugly. And maybe that is God's intention, to overcast every reflection made in night with cruelty and repulsion, because in that moment I found Verity's legs wide open, a white blanket draped indifferently over one knee. Her face nothing more than patches of black and grey shadows looking towards the ceiling. I remember painted toes clenched tight, white breasts, a jar of petroleum jelly sat orphaned beside her thigh, and the cavern of dusk between her legs where the rhythm of her hands were united in sinful, strange motions, which to my young mind left me spellbound. I shifted my weight, the move slight, but it released a short-lived creak I was sure would be lost to the noise of the mattress. But it raised above all the other noises and caused Verity to stop. Her face, veiled by night, withdrew from the ceiling and for a second or two our eyes met. I thought she was going to scream at me to get out. I thought she was going to call me horrid names and throw the pillow at me. But she didn't. Verity just looked at me. The walls of my chest resonated, the dull beat of my heart striking it like a fist. Time slowed and I was falling from another ladder. Verity finally leant her head back again into her pillow. The bed voiced its grievance once again. Feeling finally reach my legs, allowing me to slide to the floor. I rolled back to my pillow beneath the bed and waited until the noises stopped. Eventually, dawn gathered authority over night, giving everything that was once grey colour.

Another mallard takes flight from the lake. Silver jewels of water fall from its webbed feet. What was once calm in the lake is now unbalanced; what was once placid now disturbed. When I take what feels like my first breath in five minutes, similar ripples of disruption run over Prudence.

'She knew you were there, watching?'

'I wasn't watching. You make it sound perverted.'

Prudence pauses only to readjust her skirt. It's tight, short and plaid. Before I began talking about Verity, Prudence was content to allow the skirt to ride up. Now she's pushing the skirt down, trying to make it longer than it really is.

'You can see how weird that sounds?' she says.

I throw another piece of bread in the lake. This time there are no takers.

'What happened? The next day?' she asks.

'Nothing,' I say. 'I went down, had breakfast and then went to school.'

Picking at the blades of grass around her, Prudence asks, 'She didn't say anything?'

Inside my gut it feels like I've swallowed a dozen goldfish.

'I don't really recall anything being said. We just got on with our lives.'

I look out over the lake and then back to Prudence. On her lap is a nest-size mound of grass. I grab her hand, stopping her from picking up more. Prudence pulls away and stands up, wiping her skirt clean. A breeze announces itself as she walks to the edge of the embankment, fringe blown to reveal indignation in her eyes. Its breath causes her arms to clasp around her body. I follow, standing beside her.

'Has she ever…you know?'

I don't know, so I ask her to explain.

'Do I really need to spell it out?'

I take a guess at touch, or worse. I shake my head.

'She was reluctant to even offer me a hug most of the time.'

'I hear some pretty weird shit at work. We have social services pick up antiseptic cream all the time for kids, some of them of no age at all.'

'If I needed antiseptic cream, I'd probably remember why.'

'Maybe, maybe not. The mind is a powerful thing. Could be you blocked it out. A horrible experience can scramble the brain. I have to admit your mother was acting pretty fucking strange when we visited her. What was with that cigarette thing? And the way she kept staring at you while we were eating? It was weird. Then there was the way you reacted, as if you felt it too and was disgusted by it all. The way you leapt at her, it was as if you wanted to kill her. I think you would have had Taupe not entered the room.' Prudence turns to me and adds, 'Maybe you need a little time on your own, to think things through.'

'Time is something I don't have much of.'

She replies, 'You have plenty. Until you understand your past, you won't fully be able to accept your future. Look what happened to your father: he couldn't accept it either and went crazy. I can help you as much as possible, but I think you need to resolve some issues before it's too late.'

Prudence asks me to drop her off at her flat. She tells me she is only a phone call away should I need to talk, but I should take a few days alone to get my head straight.

I have a rare heart disease that is going to kill me. My mother could be a paedophile, and my girlfriend is killing off every manic depressive and lonely old pensioner with a heart problem this side of town. The only way I can get my head straight is to put a bullet through it.

CHAPTER 16

Mandrake's cackle reveals more than poor dental work: its faltering timbre holds the story of two broken marriages, a three-year stretch for GBH, and one kidney transplant. Misery follows Mandrake like the smell of shit follows a tramp. This is why I feel I'm in good company when around him. If Prudence can teach me to accept the misfortune that has come from having poor genes, then I'm quite sure Mandrake can teach me how to welcome it with open arms.

'Whatever's eating you tonight, kid, it must be really suffering,' he says.

This remark gets a showy guffaw from the barman named Campbell. The podgy-faced publican has dropped the hard man act he showed me the first time I came here two weeks ago and has now taken a kinder approach. The suspicion he held when I had a black eye is now gone. There are no uncomfortable silences, no teeth sucking. As long as I'm drinking until all common sense has left my head, and money from my pocket, he engages me in conversation. He laughs just as loud as Mandrake when I crack a joke. It's an act, one I don't mind being a part of. To have someone take an interest is worth the money.

I turn to Mandrake and tell him, 'It's nothing. Women trouble.'

'Is she fat?' asks Mandrake, and I shake my head. 'Never get involved with a fat woman. They're about as useful as window screen wiper on a goat's arsehole. Did you say she was fat?'

'She's not fat.'

'Then why you not laughing?' he asks offering me a cigarette.

I decline and tell him I have to make some real big decisions otherwise I might lose the one person that means the most to me.

Light from above the bar bounces off Mandrake's bald head

creating dark shadows in every deep fold of skin on his face. These dark lines add to his already threatening gaze, one I'm sure helped secure the verdict at his trial.

'You been caught fucking someone else?' he asks.

'No.'

'Has she?'

'No.'

'Then there's a good chance whatever it is will blow over. Stop with the doom and gloom and have another drink. You can be thankful at least she's not ugly.'

Sometimes life can be this simple. The message is so clear you don't see it until it's written out on an idiot board. I ask Mandrake to repeat what he said.

'What'aya deaf?' he asks. 'Get another drink and stop worrying. Maybe you should get me one, too. I wouldn't want to start worrying as well.'

Mandrake gives the order, and Campbell, without hesitation, starts to pull two more beers.

'Really, I've been with my fair share of hideous women,' says Mandrake. 'Some you could throw in a river and skim ugly for weeks. Some were just plain ugly. Really it's not worth the —'.

I stop him. 'She's not ugly.' I say. 'But what you said about doom and gloom, it may just have saved my relationship.'

The beers arrive and I pay Campbell. I offer to buy him one too but he refuses but keeps the change. He always does. He drops the money into a big old Mason jar beside the till. Mandrake told me the contents of the jar have been set aside for his wife. I asked Mandrake if Campbell was saving the money to buy her something nice, and Mandrake said Campbell wasn't even married. The money was to buy a wife. Campbell realised that all the money he's spent on wooing women over the years that never amounted to much, he could have bought one off the Internet. So he decided he was going to do exactly that. The only advice Mandrake gave Campbell was to make sure she wasn't Russian, because apparently Russian women have more faces than Mount Rushmore.

I reach in my pocket and pull out a few coins.

'Where's the phone?'

Campbell points to the corner of the room, a quiet and poorly lit quarter that appears as welcoming as Mandrake's smile.

'You calling her?' asks Mandrake, and I nod. 'Big mistake. You need to show her who's boss. Let her sweat a little.'

I make my way over to the phone.

I try Prudence's mobile first, but it's turned off. After several rings, she picks up at her flat.

'Who is this?' she asks.

In the background, I hear a man's voice.

'It's me,' I say.

I hear the man's voice again, deep and raspy.

'Who's that?'

'Who's who?'

'That voice. Is that a man? Is it Patrick?'

Prudence pauses and the man's voice stops.

'It's the television. Where are you?'

'In good company,' I say.

'Are you drunk?'

'What were you watching?'

'I don't know, something about Nigeria.' I'm about to say bullshit when she adds, 'This is why they tell you not to drink while taking pain killers.'

'I could run a marathon. In fact, I may just do that after I've finished speaking to you.'

'No you won't. You can hardly walk these days, let alone run.'

She's right.

'If you want to talk, meet me outside work tomorrow before nine. Now go home and sleep it off, Jack.'

And with that the phone goes dead. To not sound cowardly, I laugh at the receiver and tell its incessant tone I will not be spoken to like that anymore. With a melodramatic flourish, I slam the handset down and make my way back to the bar.

'You sort things out, kid?' asks Campbell.

'Course he did,' says Mandrake. 'The kid's a lion. He knows how to handle women, right?'

I nod and gulp more of my beer.

'See. Let her stew. Don't be a fool and ring her back. Listen to what Mandrake says.'

Another customer pulls Campbell away from the conversation. When he's out of earshot I tell Mandrake I have to run a marathon.

'Tonight?' he asks. 'Then I recommend one for the road. Best not to attempt something like that without provisions.'

We spend the rest of that drink deconstructing the world, from poverty to politics, horse racing to women. I contributed little to the discussions, but instead listen as Mandrake and Campbell speak of issues that were as important as they were challenging to resolve. Mandrake's layman philosophy is that the world is only complicated because people over think things too much. At the very heart of any problem lies a simple solution. If this is true, and that my problem lies in the heart, then the simplest solution would be to remove it. I am less than a month away from my thirtieth birthday, the day no Glass man has ever reached. No doctor, based on my family history alone, is willing to push me up the donor list because of a possible heart attack. I am not critical enough in their eyes, merely paranoid. But if I could remove that which has weakened and damaged my heart, then the problem would, for the interim at least, be halved. This is why I sit next to Mandrake with a simple smile on my face.

'Doom and Gloom,' I say under my breath.

Doom and Gloom.

CHAPTER 17

The morning streets appear to me like a watercolour painting left out in the rain. Everything is smudged and bleeding into each other. There are no defining edges to anything. No sharp corners or straight lines.

I take a seat on the bench outside the hospital doors, the same place the man with the IV drip told me my nose was bleeding.

8.49AM.

Ten more minutes left.

Like a man explaining the height of a small child, I hold my hands out before me. Each finger trembles. These hands are alien, stolen and replaced for those of a cadaver's. I tuck them under my lap to keep them warm and out of sight. To purge my lungs of Mandrake's cigarettes, and the foul stench left in my mouth by the many beers consumed the night before, I draw in the morning air, one mouthful at a time.

'You look like you've been dredged from a riverbed.'

Hair tied back into a ponytail, skin pale like fresh milk, a few buttons on her dispenser's uniform undone so you can see the perfect line of her cleavage, Prudence stands like a slutty angel before me.

I ask, 'Is having your tits on show like that for Patrick's benefit, or the Nigerian?'

'If you've come here to insult me then I'm going inside.'

I shrug. 'Do what you want.'

Prudence moves away, towards the big glass doors leading to A&E. I shout her name and she stops and walks back. She doesn't say anything but waits with one arm resting on her hip.

'Do you think it can go back to how it was?'

'What?' she asks.

'Us.'

'You remember what happened between you and Verity yet?'

'Not exactly.'

'Not exactly?'

'I don't think anything happened between us.'

Prudence takes a few steps nearer to me.

'I saw what you guys were like,' she says, voice low. 'That's not normal.'

'Look, I don't remember.'

'So what have you been doing for the past few days?'

'Drinking,' I tell her.

Prudence makes her way to the doors again.

The thought of having to raise my voice again seems less desirable than letting her go. So I do, but when the doors slide open, revealing strangers clutching bandages with worried expressions, I muster up enough strength to get one word out.

'Please!' I shout.

She stops, waits, turns and comes back again.

'You're hung over, Jack.'

I nod.

'History repeats itself, isn't that what they say?' she asks.

'Not with me.'

'I'm not convinced.'

I ask her to sit.

'Maybe I don't want to.'

I ask her again.

She lets out a sigh of resignation.

'I don't have long,' she says. 'My shift starts in five minutes.'

I tell Prudence, 'Things have changed between us. You've become colder,' I say. 'Verity has forged a gap between us, one that can't be healed until I do something about her. It's almost as if you're telling me it's you or Verity.'

'I'm not saying that, Jack.' Prudence pauses for a moment then adds, 'Is this why you can't have sex with me, because of that memory?'

'I can't because of my heart.'

'It might not be down to your heart. It might be psychological. Panic attacks spawned from that one incident when you saw Verity on the bed?'

'Freud would fucking love me.'

Prudence sits next to me and rests her hand on my lap.

'For argument's sake, let's say nothing happened between you and Verity.'

'Nothing did.'

'Right. Verity brought you up the best she knew how, but what she knew wasn't enough. Or should I say, she was robbed of what she knew.'

'I don't understand.'

'After your father died, something died in Verity. She couldn't connect on an emotional level, not to you, or your sister. The death of your father robbed her of any maternal affection. Regardless of how callous a person you are, or how closed off emotionally to those around you, every person needs an outlet. You said your father drank when he found out about his heart condition, so that was his outlet. Now you're doing the same. You told me Verity had a lot men stay over when you were a kid, yet she's never settled down with anyone or re-married. Sex is Verity's outlet: she allows her body to be used because in return she feels connected. Now, for argument's sake, let's say all this is true. The way she acted with you the other night, it's just her way of connecting to you. She doesn't know any different.'

'You think?'

'It's possible. There's another possibility of course, which, added to the first, makes more sense. Have you ever heard of borderline personality disorder?'

I shake my head.

'I know enough to think your mother may have it.'

I ask if borderline personality disorder is the reason she's acting the way she is, and Prudence says, 'All I know is the patient usually follows a set pattern of bad relationships, and the only thing that exists to them is joylessness. Everything else, the world around them, the people, their family, they're secondary. A person with this disorder holds no compassion or love. It would explain her detachment.'

There's that word again, detachment.

'So she's just miserable?' I explain.

'Misery is a factor, bitterness another. Could be she wanted you to experience this world she lives in. Verity probably feels better when she's fucking with your head and causing conflict. Misery loves company and all that shit.'

'So it has nothing to do with sex? The way she's acting is down to some deep-rooted anxiety spawned from the death of my father?'

'Look, I don't know for sure. But her phobias are a contributing factor to her character, and part of her way of dealing with them is to use sex as a control mechanism. Verity can't address her feelings like any other normal parent. She has become re-programmed into thinking sex is the only way to connect to the outside world, a world beyond her phobias, which means, there is a very good chance something may have happened to you. I'm not saying it was sex, but there was probably a time when even she didn't understand the consequence of her actions. She was probably lonely and just wanted to bond with you.'

A boy used to fill the void left behind by a dead husband. Contact.

Prudence looks out towards the big glass doors and shakes her head, eyes resting on an empty space in front of her.

'I can't believe the amount of misery that woman has given you over the years. You had every right to want to kill her. Christ, I'd have done the same.'

'I wanted to tell you last night,' I say. 'I understand now how to make things right, between us, and Verity.'

She turns back and says, 'You and I are fine, Jack, but if you think I'm going to speak to that bitch again you're sadly —'

I press my finger against her lips. I tell her she will talk to Verity again. She has to.

'Do you still have the flyer Verity gave you?' I ask her.

'For Taupe's band? What about it?'

'Do you still have it?'

'Yes, but I don't understand how going to see a band will help you overcome the issues you have.'

'Music isn't the answer. It's a message,' I say. 'Verity wants to be absolved for her sins. She wants to be free from her phobias.'

'I have no idea what you're talking about, Jack.'

'The name of the band, do you remember it?'

Prudence thinks back, and says, 'Mattress something.'

'Matricide,' I say.

Prudence's eyes thaw. Her lips thin to a smile. The indifference fashioned by doubt has gone. In its place the warmness of trust brings colour to her cheeks. I'm no longer a stranger, nor a freak with an Oedipus Complex. I'm the man she cares about, a man who can only overcome his fear of death through the act of murder.

CHAPTER 18

'Take the biggest breath you can,' says Mandrake. 'Hold it. When you let it out, I want to hear you count.'

He takes a swig from his glass and gestures with his hand for me to begin.

Lungs inflate, ribs ache. I hold and then let it out.

'One, two, three, four, five…'

I look to Mandrake for approval but he's motioning to Campbell for two more drinks.

'Six, seven, eight, nine, ten...'

'You know it could be just guilt,' he says, pulling out a fiver and placing it on the bar. 'Remember what I told you about those Egyptians?'

I nod.

'Fifteen, sixteen, seventeen...'

'A heart so light must be pure, but a heart so heavy must be weighed down with sin and evil? You remember that?'

I nod again.

'Twenty three, twenty four, twenty five …'

'All I'm saying is a heart can also be weighed down with guilt, too.'

My chest burns white hot.

'Could explain things, you know? Anxiety attacks, I mean.'

'Forty six, forty seven, forty eight...'

'How you doing?' he asks.

I nod my head to say I'm fine.

What Mandrake doesn't know is my chest feels like fat man's knee is being forced deep into its centre and that my eyes are close to popping out of my skull. What Mandrake doesn't know is how close he is to the truth.

Campbell places the drinks on the counter and looks at me. Both he and Mandrake are transfixed with something on my forehead, which I assume is either a distended vein, or the colour of skin.

Before I reach eighty seven, I fill my insides again with the pub's dank air.

'Eighty six,' Mandrake confirms. 'See, proves there's nothing wrong. People with lung cancer, emphysema or asthma, they only reach forty at best. Now stop worrying.'

Between heavy breaths, I ask, 'You think my shortness of breath is just down to guilt?'

'It sure isn't anything to do with your lungs.'

Campbell takes the money off the bar and tills it in. He hands Mandrake the change and asks me what I have to feel guilty for. If racing through numbers helps measure the state of your lungs, then maybe going through all the shit in my life will help measure the shame.

'Kid, you've been coming here for some time now,' says Campbell, 'and you always look like you're carrying the weight of the world on your shoulders. What is it?'

Euthanasia.

Chastity.

Incest.

Across the room, an old couple muffled by age whisper to each other. Sat close to them are three men playing dominoes, faces crooked by boredom, or possibly the familiarity of company. In the corner, a middle-aged man dressed in work overalls stares blankly into his drink, lost to his past, or maybe just apprehensive towards his future. And as I watch these people torn between discomfort and tolerance, I remember that only a few weeks ago, I walked in this room and felt similarly; I too was lost and abandoned. Here, those with bad luck and failing organs bide their time quietly in similar company until the inevitable happens. What Campbell offers here is more than alcohol and shelter; to the disheartened he gives respite from their worries, and like his patrons I attend not because I have nothing better to do, but out of necessity. Death is no picnic, but melancholy is definitely the hors d'oeuvre. Campbell, the sycophantic publican, Mandrake, the ex-con; they have shown me more compassion and understanding, and given me more advice about bettering my life than my mother did in all the years we shared the same house. If they wish to know why I carry the weight of the world on my shoulders, they have earned the right to know the truth. This public house shares its pain, soaks it into every fixture, bleeds it deep into the wood grain on the bar so everyone can be reminded someone is much worse off. If I share this pain, my guilt, would it then be evermore imprinted too? Would my suffering help other people in their moment of wretchedness?

Mandrake sees my pain. He understands, like the priest and Prudence, the saint and the sinner. I smile at him. In return, more creases branch across his face, more decaying teeth exposed, eyes, indignant, twinkle with understanding.

He looks to Campbell and says, 'You ever thought the kid comes here just for your charming repartee?'

Campbell chews on Mandrake's suggestion, the white pasty flesh of his chin more prominent with every second that passes. With almost perfect timing, he rearranges an askew beer towel and tells Mandrake and myself, 'Not fucking likely.'

We all laugh, and for a moment nothing matters, nothing in the world.

Distraction.

Campbell then goes off to serve another customer, another lost soul, and Mandrake and I return to our pints. Without the banter, I'm left falling helplessly back into reality where my thoughts are as jagged as thorns, each one tearing into my brain. I order another drink for both Mandrake and myself. One more. One more is all I need. Then I can go face Verity. One more drink, and I'll be another minute closer to removing at least one of those thorns.

CHAPTER 19

A ghostly apparition in a cabinet mirror grips my throat. It takes me aback until I realise it's my own reflection. I look five days away from having every orifice in my body filled with cotton wadding and embalming fluid pumped into my veins. Foundation cream would do nothing for my complexion right now. I swing back the cabinet's door, pick up a tube of Clotrimazole, squeeze some onto my fingers, smell it and put it back next to a container of cotton buds. Wiping my fingers clean, I notice a white bottle with a pharmacist instructional label: Migril. The medical reference book from inside my jacket tells me it's used for migraines.

The symptoms of an overdose: vomiting, diarrhoea, thirst, tingling, itching, cold skin, rapid weak pulse, confusion, coma.

I spill out ten tablets into my palm, put them in my trouser pocket and return to searching the cabinet.

Another brown pharmacy bottle: Amytal (Amylobarbitine). I flick open the book. Sedative. Grey fingers scroll down the possible complications one might expect if the patient takes too many: Low blood pressure, coma, cessation of breathing, death may occur.

Muffled laughter breaches the floorboard beneath my feet. I empty the entire contents of the bottle into my pocket, shut the cabinet, flush the toilet and make my way downstairs.

Before entering the living room, I place my coat on a hook in the hall and brush my hands over my hair to straighten it. Deep breath. Making sure the book is hidden in the coat, I return back to the living room.

Prudence is sat with legs crossed on the arm of my chair. She's too busy responding to something Verity said to notice me walk back in.

'I find mixing in a little coconut oil makes the skin a little softer,' Verity says. 'It helps reduce the appearance of stretch marks.'

Prudence nods as if taking mental notes.

'Prudence was telling me your cardiologist has put you on new medication,' Verity says. 'Is it helping?'

I sit next to Prudence, feel her elbow nudge my ribs. I nod my head in agreement.

'That's good,' says Verity. She turns to Prudence and adds, 'It must be hard, knowing about the condition. Puts a strain on the relationship.'

'Not so much,' Prudence replies. 'We're working our lives around it instead of the other way around. Besides, it makes us both treasure every solitary second we have together.'

Prudence hugs me with her one free arm and I play the words over in my head. I wonder how much of what she said is acting and how much is truth.

Verity says, 'I just wish the same was true in my marriage.'

Verity is wearing a short cut v-neck T-shirt with Rolling Stones lip print, a denim miniskirt, fishnet tights and red stilettos. I don't have any memory of Verity dressing conservatively, which leads me to conclude any problems with her marriage to my father might not have been solely contributed to his drinking and heart condition.

'What was Mr Glass like?' asks Prudence.

Verity pauses, rubbing her finger along the side of her glass to clear a long streak of condensation.

'Quiet. But people liked him.'

She takes the glass to her lips and drinks the contents in one. Her throat moves like a snake's body consuming a mouse. When finished, she asks us both if we would like a fill up. I tell her I'm fine. Prudence makes an effort to finish her drink of cranberry juice and vodka. Once done she holds out her glass for Verity to take.

When Verity is out of the room, Prudence says to me, 'Find anything?'

I reach into my trouser pocket and pull out the tablets. Prudence holds them in her hands and looks at them like a jeweller appraising diamonds.

'Amytal and Migril,' I tell her.

'Nice,' she says.

'There was cream, too, Clotrimazole.'

'That's no good. It's used for thrush,' she says.

I rub my fingers on the side of the couch.

Verity shouts from the kitchen and Prudence slips the tablets into her cardigan's pocket. Today, Prudence is going for responsible: ankle length black skirt, pastel-blue cardigan and white T-shirt.

Poking her head from behind the door, Verity says, 'I said, do you want anything to eat? The lasagne is going to take another forty minutes at least. I've got crab cakes?'

Both Prudence and I look to each other, a wry little smirk forming on both our faces.

'I'm fine,' I say.

'Maybe just the one, then,' says Prudence. 'I have to watch my figure.'

'Honey, please. You're no thicker than willow branch,' says Verity before disappearing back into the kitchen.

I ask Prudence what she's playing at.

'I don't know what you mean, Mr Rydal?' she says.

'You know what I mean. And I don't want to be someone else today. Today I'm me. For once, I need to be myself.'

'Fine,' she says. 'Just stop acting so jittery. Do you want Verity to realise something's up?'

Verity walks back into the room and hands Prudence a small plate, fork and a refilled glass of Cranberry juice and vodka.

'I bought a whole lot of those crab cakes yesterday,' she says taking her seat, 'but Henry and the boys ate most of them last night.'

'How is Henry?' asks Prudence.

'He's fine. I won't see him till tomorrow though. He's got the lads booked into a student gig in town tonight. At my age, it gets pretty damn lonely at night. How's that crab?'

Prudence nods and makes a sound a yummy sound.

'They're a little too rich for me.' Prudence says. 'They bring on migraines, and as you can imagine, I don't care for such things when I know I'm seeing Henry.'

I pick up the glass of wine next to me and neck its content.

'Thirsty?' asks Verity.

'Do you have anything stronger?' I ask.

'We may have some whiskey in the cupboard above the sink.'

Verity gets up to fetch me a glass. I raise my hand and tell her

I'll go instead.

Tinted by a dusk sun settling beyond the window, everything in the kitchen is cast in shades of orange and yellow. I take a kitchen knife from one of the drawers and lift up my shirtsleeve. Skin is jaundice, broken by fine dark hairs and green veins. The knife refracts light as good as any prism, casting a white shark-like shape across my chest, then arm. I tease the flesh with the edge of the blade, then, like a violinist advancing a bow along delicate strings, I draw one long stroke of the knife upward, then back down again, scoring a line across my forearm until the blade gathers red with blood. I run it over my tongue and taste machinery parts. Kitchen towel acts as a bandage. I pull my sleeve down and search the cupboard above the sink. A cheap bottle of whisky sits orphaned on a shelf, the name of which I have never heard.

Silence is the fourth person in the room when I enter. Prudence is wiping her mouth clean and placing the empty plate next to the chair. Verity is examining black fingernails, picking at the dirt resting beneath. Taking my seat, Prudence signals me to initiate a conversation. The best I can do is ask about Anne Marie.

'Busy, with work,' says Verity. 'Did you hear she's been promoted to team leader?'

I didn't know this. I don't even know what Anne Marie does. It's been so long since we spoke.

'She's doing very well,' says Verity. 'Both her and Ian are thinking about tying the knot next year, all going well. She wants a big white wedding, told me as much last time she called. Monday I think?' she says to herself. 'Could have been Tuesday. I forget when. She said she'd been to the grave too and put some flowers on there for your father's birthday.'

'You never told me it was your father's birthday,' says Prudence.

'It wasn't,' I tell her, and watch as the weight of guilt sinks Verity into her chair.

'So how did you guys meet?' Verity asks, changing the subject.

'Work,' Prudence says. 'I'm a dispenser in the local hospital. Repeat prescriptions does wonders for breaking the ice.'

'Really?'

'Oh yeah, you'd be surprised how friendly and relaxed people get when you're keeping them alive. They'll tell you anything.'

I rest my hand on Prudence's knee, squeezing it gently.

'I don't think my mother is interested in —'

Verity interjects, 'No, that's okay, I find it interesting.'

A long monologue of incidents and anecdotes follows forcing me to grip tight the part of my arm cut by the knife. When Prudence slows to take a breath, the sting from beneath my shirtsleeve has developed into an unbearable throbbing.

'You must be able to get your hands on most things?' asks Verity, the subtext reading like a covert conversation between two drug dealers.

'High-end medication, like morphine, or sedatives, they're all numbered and under lock and key. If a patient needs any of this, I need approval from the pharmacist who then unlocks the cabinet. It's all very thorough. Stuff like ointment though, like thrush cream say, I can hand them out without going through any procedures.'

For a second the throbbing in my arm subsides long enough for me to cherish each dilated pupil in Verity's eyes, the crimson blush that warms her corpse like skin, and the apprehension that precedes embarrassment.

'I'll go check on the lasagne,' she says getting to her feet. Before walking out, she turns to us, her forehead gathered in pleats. 'I never thought to ask, but are you okay with lasagne?'

Verity has already asked this question when we arrived, and while both Prudence and I agree once again, to witness Verity left disorientated by Prudence's gibe is wonderfully satisfying, a feeling which overrules that of the pain in my arm. It allows me to return to the room, and to the reason I am here. For a moment at least, I am without guilt or reservation towards ending my mother's life.

The lasagne is dry and the cheese is burnt. Every mouthful makes me heave. No one has spoke since Verity put this shit out for us to eat. It's so quiet around the table all I hear is the clink of knife scoring porcelain, the squelching sound of Verity's tongue and the dull groan from my stomach as the food is digested.

'You've lost weight,' Verity says to me.

I look down at my fingers, long like stalagmites.

'Is he eating?' she asks Prudence.

'When I'm around he does,' she says.

The concerned girlfriend.

'I could make you meals. Drop them off from time to time. You have a microwave, right?'

'There's no need,' I say. 'Just run down is all.'

'Before you go, remind me to give you some vitamins. I have bottles of the stuff in the kitchen I never use.'

Time strives to make headway. I am conscious its efforts will be hindered by Prudence's need to finish her meal so she can offer her services. What Prudence wants right now is for us all to be drinking coffee. I look at my plate and there are at least ten mouthfuls left until that very moment. To moisten the lasagne in my mouth I take a mouthful of whisky. When finished, I ask for another and Prudence looks to me, a deep frown developing over her eyes.

'I'll get it,' says Verity.

When she's gone Prudence turns to me and asks, 'What the hell is the matter with you?'

'Nothing,' I say, 'but this room seems a little unsure of itself.'

'You're drunk,' Prudence says.

'I've been drunk before. This is most definitely boarding on merry. In an hour, ask the question again and you'll get a much different answer.'

'You need to focus. You need to forget everything, your history —'

I place my hand in front of her face.

'Save me the melodramatic coaching process,' I say. 'I know the spiel off by heart.'

Her hand rests on mine, face ruined by shadows.

'We can finish the meal and get a taxi back to your place. There'll be other times, better times to do this.'

'But tomorrow always seems better yesterday,' I whisper to her.

'I don't think you're ready. Not for this. Not now,' she says.

'I never will be.'

Verity returns and hands me the glass of whiskey.

'You like the boys in the band?' I ask Verity as she sits down. 'How old is the average member of the band? Young, I bet.'

Prudence forces out a theatrical laugh that startles me, knocking the glass of whiskey across the table.

'Oh, honey, you are clumsy,' Prudence says, dabbing it with a serviette.

Sheets of pasta and hard cheese soak up the whiskey like a desert flower.

'That's okay, really. Let me,' Verity says, applying her serviette in the same frantic manner as Prudence.

'I think it's safe to say your dinner is ruined,' Verity says.

'I don't think the whiskey was a major factor in that,' I say, and the back of Prudence's hand strikes my arm. Rubbing it, I look up and see her teeth exposed like a perfect dental mould.

'You're being rude,' she says, teeth gritted, tone pleasant and amiable.

'I never was one for cooking,' says Verity.

Roll back fifteen years: From what I can recall, we were champions of the fast food outlets, kings of the TV dinner meals. I think about all the saturated fat, all the cholesterol, salt and sugar in those meals. Is it any wonder my heart is failing?

I watch whiskey descend over the edge of the table: drip, drip, drip. It lands on my knee creating an island of charcoal-grey on my trousers.

'I'll get you some fresh,' Verity says taking the plate away.

'Don't bother. It was an abomination, like most things you produce, myself included.'

I hear Prudence sigh.

'What's going on?' Verity asks.

She takes her seat again and places the plate back on the table. Prudence twists the serviette in her hands, face pensive. An offer is made for coffee, effort given to emphasise her proposal to me. Prudence wants to know if it's okay to bring an end to this.

'Another whisky for me, dear,' I say.

Verity, refusing to look elsewhere but my eyes, says to Prudence, 'I'll have a coffee, sure.'

When Prudence is out of the room, Verity picks up a cigarette from the box, lights it, and says, 'You want to tell me what's on your mind?'

The flare from the lighter lifts the sombre pall from her face, and all at once the moment becomes still framed; eyes wide, vulnerable, skin smoothed out like fresh plaster. She flicks the lighter closed and light deadens to a veil of blue smoke.

'You really want to know what's wrong?'

'I wouldn't have asked otherwise.'

'You.'

She sucks back on the smoke. A second or two later it leaves her mouth, weakened.

'Meaning?' she asks.

I shift my weight on the chair.

'Remember?'

'Remember what?'
'When you failed,' I say.
'I don't understand.'
'At being a mother.'

She looks for an answer in my eyes, smoke twisting up to the ceiling like Indian rope. She takes a drag from the cigarette, eyes drawn to her mouth, one I am sure has been a receptacle for many a man's seed.

'I've never confessed to being a great mother,' she says. 'I know I've been hard on you at times, and I don't blame your hostility, but losing your father was hard for me, too. Raising two kids was hard.'

I remember a time she used a distraction technique to stop me from crying. Taking her thumb from one hand, she would bend it at the knuckle, join it to the opposite thumb and then slide it along her index finger. The desired effect made the thumb appear to detach itself from the knuckle. It was a trick, a lousy one at that, but at the time it made me laugh. Somewhere in me I know there were more times like that, more times when she tried. And for a moment I reign in the deep-rooted hate towards her in exchange for compassion. But it is fleeting and nothing comes of it, my past is in fragmentation, the gaps plugged with ill will.

'You still like Linda Ronstadt?' I ask.

'You remember her?'

'You had all her records, under your bed.'

'I threw them away years ago. Sometimes you have to let go of the past,' she says.

'Shame the same can't be done with memories.'

'Say it. Whatever it is, say it. I'm sure you'll feel better and we won't need to go through these silly mind games.'

I laugh. A little vomit sits at the back of my throat.

'Mind games,' I say.

'Look, if you want me to say I could have been a better mother, I will. But I won't start dredging up incidents one by one so you can watch me squirm. We all have parts of our life we wish we could erase, but we can't. I know it's easier for a child to pin all their faults, their anxieties and flaws on their parents. I get that. But there comes a time when the child has to take responsibility and make changes to better their own life. They have to take action.'

From the kitchen I hear the tapping of a metal spoon on porcelain. Prudence has already crushed the tablets. Good old

Prudence.

Verity leans back in her chair, blowing smoke to the ceiling: half laugh, half sigh.

'Why didn't you treat me like a normal son? Why did you cross that line?'

'Jesus Christ, Jack. What line did I cross? I treated you the same as I treated Anne Marie, no different.'

'Bullshit.'

Verity pulls her chair from the table and stands up.

'I don't need to hear this shit from you. You think you're the only one been hard done by? You think you're the only one in pain? You never lost the one person you loved. You never spent nights realising your life was over before it'd begun. You don't know what it was like to think you're better off not living!'

Words settle around us, some burning in the flame of the candle, some resting on skin. Her eyes travel beyond the walls, her mind a thousand days reflecting.

'I have,' I say. 'These past few months I have thought of nothing else.'

Prudence walks in, two cups in her hands.

'Everything okay?' she asks to no one in particular.

Verity looks at me, chest rising like restless waves. My stomach burns cold, every muscle soft and tender. I try to remember to breathe, to keep everything functioning as it should.

Verity sits back down and Prudence hands her a cup. She tells Verity she didn't know if she took sugar. Verity says no. Prudence places the other cup down on a coaster in front of her plate and walks back into the kitchen.

Nothing is said in her absence.

When she returns, Prudence hands me a tumbler of whisky. I take a large swig and place it down in front of me, eyes settling on the glass.

'Do you know what all this is about?' Verity asks Prudence.

Pause.

'A little,' she says.

'Care to tell me?'

Prudence arranges her knife and fork.

'I don't think it's for me to say.'

Without looking at her, I feel Verity staring at me.

'Thought as much.'

Steam rises from Verity's coffee cup. I look to Prudence and she smiles to tell me everything will be okay.

I grip my glass and finish the contents in one.

'Ready now?' Verity asks me.

'Do you have feelings for me, more than maternal?' I ask.

She laughs.

'You're really fucked up, aren't you?' she says, and continues laughing.

'I don't think this is very funny,' Prudence says. 'Your son has carried this around with him for so long, the least you can do is hear him out.'

Verity picks up the coffee cup and takes a few sips, the aftertaste bringing some displeasure to her face. Verity swirls her little finger around the rim of the cup. Prudence sees this and clears her throat.

'It tastes funny,' Verity says.

'Could be the milk was nearing its sell by?' explains Prudence.

'I bought fresh today.'

Verity's little finger is picking out dandruff size spots of crushed Amytal and Migril, her black painted nail hovering under her nose. The warm rosy flesh of her tongue pushes out, resting on her bottom lip: the nail moving closer to it.

Prudence screams.

There's blood on my hands, black and thick. Plates and glasses are on the floor, the strong smell of coffee close by. My arm is wet, elbow throbbing. I know a piece of glass is stuck in my arm without even looking.

'This is bad!' Prudence says, her words landing over me like rustic leaves falling from an autumn tree. 'We're not even wearing gloves!'

On the floor, a few inches from me, and draped over the upturned chair, two legs bound in denim and fishnets twitch, a pool of blood already swelling beside the head. Prudence has stopped talking leaving the sound of gurgling to fill the silence. I pull myself off the table and see Verity holding her throat, a bloodied fork sticking from its centre, her pulse visible as more blood beats out from around its handle.

'This is bad,' Prudence repeats

'I…' is all I can say.

'This is so bad.'

'What do we do?'

While the gravity of my fury lies personified in the act of murder, I welcome the noise of oozing blood from my mother's throat that punctuates the silence around us. Any noise, even those of my mother's final breath, helps lift the hopelessness I feel right now.

When Prudence finally speaks, her voice is soft and low, 'We do what we came here to do,' she says. Forcing my hand out towards Verity, she says, 'We learn.'

I kneel down, blood seeping through my trousers, warm as syrup. Verity follows my eyes. Small gasps of her fetid breath spoil the air around her. I glance at the fork in her throat. I can't see any of its prongs, just the curve where the handle meets the head. It must have gone all the way through to the other side, no doubt pressed tight against the spinal cord. She looks like she's wearing a rose corsage on her neck.

'You'll have to check her radial pulse, like with Ilse,' says Prudence.

'What's the other method?'

'The carotid pulse. But it's located in the neck.'

'I want to feel that pulse,' I tell Prudence.

'They're both the same, honey. Besides, I don't —'

I cut her off and repeat what I just told her.

Prudence kneels down beside me, making sure she doesn't get any blood on her shoes.

I feel her hand on my shoulder.

'Take your second and third finger, like I've shown you, and run them alongside the outer edge of the trachea.'

I reach over, fingers hovering over the fork.

'You best hurry,' Prudence says. 'Her breathing is slowing down.'

The blood is thick and warm against my skin. I push each finger down and slide them against the side of Verity's windpipe.

'I can't feel anything,' I tell Prudence.

'It's near the underside of the jaw. Try going up instead of down.'

I do. It causes more blood to collect on my fingers.

At that moment, Verity's hand grips tight my wrist causing Prudence to move back and let out a scream.

'Fuck! That scared the shit out of me,' says Prudence, a little laughter seeping through as the statement tapers.

I prise Verity's fingers off my wrists. They come away quite easily. I place it on her chest.

'Are you okay?' Prudence asks me. 'That was some freaky shit. Like some horror movie.'

I tell Prudence to be quiet.

There is a dying beat, fading. I look to Prudence and nod my head.

'Remember to stay focused on the pulse, and more importantly, her eyes. You'll see it soon. You'll see how peaceful death can be.'

Everything dissolves away.

Prudence is just an echo, a memory at best. All that remains in the room is Verity and I, cradled in a black hand. I draw my face close to her. The ebb and flow of blood is slowing. In the distance, Prudence reminds me to stay focused on her eyes.

'Her pulse and eyes', comes her voice from the dark, ricocheted from a world that feels so far from me right now.

I bring my lips to Verity's ear and whisper, 'What do you see? Is it really so peaceful like Prudence says?'

Her eyelids begin to relax. The furrows in her brow iron out. My fingers count the beats in her neck. When the distant between each is too far to measure, I find myself kissing her cheek, my vision blurring as tears roll.

Pulling my fingers away, I look to Prudence.

'It's over,' I tell her.

Prudence extends a gesture of compassion, but I sense she's more relieved than anything else. Prudence goes to embrace me. I exhibit my palms so we don't touch.

'I don't want to get blood on you,' I say, and she nods.

Verity's eyes remain wide, mouth smeared red. There was the belief Verity would let me know something different than the other casualties of my distraction. But the slipping grip of life appears reliably consistent; a fade-out to black; a gentle serenity after agony. It could be that following a brief struggle where the body and mind pull against all odds to remain rooted to this shithole we call life, pain finally dissipates leaving absolute peace, freedom. It could be that the very last beat of the heart is wonderful.

'We need to clean up this place,' Prudence says.

I nod and cuff my eyes.

'Most of her blood is contained to the rug.'

'She was going to find out,' I say.

'I know she was. You did the right thing. What you did was for us.'

'And the body?'

'I don't know.'

For a moment, we both stare at Verity like she's a lost child in a busy shopping arcade, both of us unprepared for the responsibility.

'Can't we throw her in a river?'

'She'll be found. We don't want that.'

'The hospital incinerator?'

'That's okay for small things, but a whole body? Even if we hack her up, I'm quite sure it'd take a few visits. That's attention we don't need.'

Just the thought of cutting Verity causes me to dry retch.

'We can't afford to have your vomit on this carpet as well.'

'What do you think Harold will say?'

'What do you care? Going off her reputation, the chances are he'll think she's run off with someone else. If not, then you'll have to convince him of that.'

'Me?'

'People are going to call asking about Verity. And what are you going to say?'

I look to Verity again. The blood looks thicker, darker in the aftermath of death.

'I don't know.'

'You tell them you've not seen her. You talked on the phone and you made arrangements to come visit Saturday, but you cancelled. You tell them I was sick, that you wanted to make sure I was okay. Give me your phone.'

I reach into my jacket and hand her my mobile.

'What are doing?'

'Adding credibility to your story,' she says flicking through the menus.

A few seconds later and the phone rings next to us. Upon hearing it, my heart tries to break out of my chest.

'Don't worry, it's just me,' she says picking up the receiver with the sleeve of her cardigan. She holds both phones in either hand.

'It's a little late in the day for cancelling, but at least it'll show up on any phone records.'

All the misgivings towards Prudence's actions are remedied

when convinced of their logic. All those times my thoughts wandered to the uncertainty of our motives, Prudence made clear their reasoning. She has never left me to worry unnecessarily. This is why I know she'll resolve this mess. And I'm equally confident she'll find asylum for all my worries.

'I have an idea,' she says.

CHAPTER 20

In darkness, every small sound is amplified. Leaves coalesce and roar like angry crowds. The simple dip and rise of a branch screams out its pain. This can only explain why each footstep Prudence and I take sounds as heavy as those made by horses. And why the plastic sheet I'm holding under my arm flaps as loud as wings on an albatross.

'How much further?' Prudence asks, her breath visible in streams.

'When you see Reginald Cowen, we're there.'

She looks down at the headstones below her feet, knuckles bone-white offset against the blood-soaked rug we both hold.

'It's too dark to see,' she says.

It is, but not dark enough I can't make out the rectory. The absence of light dyes every pane of glass black, and as I drag the contents of the rug through its grounds, my thoughts wander again to the priest. Is he asleep, and if so, would he be dreaming like a normal man? Do men committed to the cloth have different dreams to the rest of us, like those born blind? Perhaps they dream of charitable acts or incidents where they suffer for the greater good. Perhaps their dreams ascend beyond this mortal plain and crossover into the eternal where they converse with archangels and the poor souls they have committed to the ground. Is it conceivable to believe they may even find themselves talking to God? I have seen death dull the eyes of many, including my mother, but to see someone return from that dream and enlightened by it, well, that would be something very special.

Prudence picks up the pace causing the plastic sheet to slip from under my arm.

'This is killing me,' I say.

'I'm sorry, but I want to get this done.'

The cold air has seared the back of my throat by the time we reach my father's grave.

Holding her sides, Prudence says, 'I'll go back to the car...to get the rest of the things... Keys?'

I reach into my pocket and throw the car keys to her, a perfect aim, hitting dead centre at chest height. All the same, my precision is compromised by a poor catch and they hit the ground with the sound of a thousand horseshoes falling off a cart.

'You'll wake the dead,' I whisper.

'It's my fingers. They're frozen,' she says picking up the keys and heading back to the car. Night devours her, leaving behind the empty noise of her shoes and the thin reed of my breath.

I spend a moment looking out beyond the graveyard to where strings of tiny orange and white lights twinkle on the horizon of my hometown. If there's light, I know there is a light bulb. If there's a light bulb, I know close by there is a switch, one screwed into a wall inside a home, a home where people gather around a television and watch other people playacting, existing, loving, and dying. Not many could comprehend that only a few miles away a man is leaning on a headstone, weary and breathless from carrying his murdered mother to an empty grave. They slurp their tea and dip their bourbons, blissfully ignorant to the fact that somewhere a woman is being raped, a child beaten within an inch of their life, a noose tied with trembling hands, a whole bottle of pills opened and ingested, or the skin of a naked wrist is being scored by a razor blade. They would never think to turn off their TV if an ambulance passed their window, because there is no reason to concern themselves with those who have caused the sirens to ring aloud. Who wants to reflect on the certainty that someone is dying when it is easier to turn over the channel and watch a sickly sitcom where people drink coffee and fall out of love? Disowning truth is sometimes the only way people can exist, just as I did many years ago. When my future was untouched by chance, I was happy to be oblivious to the horrors of the real world. I did not give a second thought to the killers, paedophiles, psychos and crazies who existed outside my door. I did not give thought to Verity, nor the night I saw her on the bed. I lived my life free from these things because it made sense to. But now I am one of the horrors of life. I am the hand that stretches out of the shadow to hold the screams of a stricken woman; I am the blade thrust deep into the stomach of a teenager; I am the boot that crushes the head of a dying pigeon.

I turn to see Prudence holding two shovels.

Handing me one she says, 'Pretty, aren't they?'

'What?'

'The lights: they look pretty from afar?'

I shrug.

'How you feeling?'

'A little better,' I say.

'Good, because we need to dig.'

To hide a dead body, you need to put it in the one place no one will ever look. Prudence told me this while rolling Verity into the rug, the top of her head and feet the only parts of her visible from opposite ends. A pig in the blanket.

While wiping down the table, the free standing display cabinet containing tribal masks and native wooden bowls, Prudence asked about my father's grave, if it's true what I told her about it being empty. In the kitchen, washing cutlery, plates, glasses and coffee cups, she asked me if anyone patrols the graveyard at night.

"An old priest lives in the rectory adjacent to the graveyard," I said, and suddenly all concern left her face.

Grabbing a suitcase off the top of the wardrobe and filling it with Verity's clothes, she told me to look for a plastic sheet and two shovels. Four small stones from an adjacent grave now hold down each end of that plastic sheet. Prudence doesn't want any mistakes. I don't blame her.

'All the soil we take out needs to stay on that sheet. We have to return things to how they were.'

I'm assuming she means the grave, not life before I committed matricide. Taking her shovel, Prudence begins cutting a rectangle shape in front of the headstone, one bigger than the roll of carpet.

Sliding the shovel beneath the earth, she says, 'This is a sunken grave.'

'What do you mean?' I ask.

'There's a body in here.'

'Impossible,' I tell her. 'It's vacant, a distraction. A thumb trick at best.'

'See how the centre of the grave sags? That's due to the first body rotting away.'

She's right. The ground is indented as if an invisible coffin is lay upon it.

'Don't they recycle the earth?' I ask. 'Like, if the lease on the grave expires and the family don't renew it, don't they use the plot for a fresh body? It must be one of them, one of the old dead.'

'I'm just letting you know,' she says forcing the spade underneath the lip of the earth again. 'You might want to prepare yourself once we get down there.'

The grass works loose allowing Prudence to start rolling it up, tight like the rug next to my feet.

Out of breath, she says, 'I always wanted a garden.'

To stop the stench of a rotting corpse raising suspicion, you don't have to go further than three feet.

'Four foot will do,' she tells me.

I stand, watching in awe, a headache stirring in the deepest part of my brain.

'I'm not too sure I can dig that much soil out of the ground.'

'You only have to do about two feet, I'll do the rest.'

Six-inches down, I strike a stone with the shovel. The pain above my eye swells to the size of a golf ball. By the time we're both knee deep, the dull ache feels the size of a lemon. A cold wind dances between us. I stop a while and sit on the lip of the grave. Prudence has primitive war marks where she's wiped her brow with a dirty hand. She looks so at ease with the situation, like a child digging sandcastles or planting a tree, not at all nervous considering what we're doing.

'You did the right thing,' she says noticing me looking. 'She would have found out.'

'I wished I smoked,' I say.

Prudence stops digging and rests her arms on the shovel's handle.

'What did you see… in her eyes?'

I am knelt beside Verity again. I read the human eye remains the same size from birth, but in those final minutes preceding her death, I was sure I saw Verity's grow a little. From within the nebula of her iris, the pupil blossomed into a dark void that appeared so large I felt I could crawl into it. There was nothing to suggest she was suffering or that she was petrified, merely that the eye was growing to accommodate a much bigger vision. There are many who believe that death throws a sack over our head that provides an everlasting blindness. Our bodies rot and the only thing that ascends to the Heavens is the wailing of our family. But I have seen the grounding of God's incitement. Our bodies are too fragile for him, our vision too restricted. In Verity I saw a reaction to this change. She was preparing for another place, adjusting to a world less constrained.

'Hope,' I say.

Prudence smiles and commences digging again.

'We have a few hours before it gets light. Let's not waste it.'

I pick up my shovel and begin hacking at the soil, slower than Prudence, mindful of my heart.

Three-feet down and the soil becomes clay.

'This is impossible for two people,' I tell her.

'This is how graves were dug back in the day,' she says. 'They would dig the ground with spades, and then every couple of feet, secure the sides with shores.'

'Shores?'

'Wooden supports so the soil wouldn't fall in on them.'

Walls fashioned from dark peat and the orange clay lit by moonlight provides the only support to our grave.

To the beat of the shovel's head, Prudence recites her learning, 'A strong man could dig a six-foot grave in about three hours. They would collect soil in one corner of the grave, using it like a step so they could get out. The shores would run around them like a wooden cage, protecting them. When it came to the burial, the coffin would be lowered and remain there until all the mourners left. The same guy who dug the hole would start filling the grave back up, inch-by-inch, removing the timber shores as the grave filled. They called it donkeywork, hard graft. But it took a special kind of man to do that job, one prepared to suffer in all weathers to make sure the dead remained at peace. Now they use small petrol motored diggers with big shovels to scoop the earth up. It takes less than half that time now.'

I ask, 'You speaking from experience?'

Prudence rests her shovel on the side of the grave. Wiping the sweat from her brow, she says, 'There's a story for another day. Come on. We don't have much time.'

Below ground level, the smell of death is always on you. It's only the sound of your breath, the soil being sliced, and the faint rumble of life beyond, which affirms you're not.

'Told you,' Prudence says.

I look to where she is pointing. Fragments of a broken skull lay sprayed around her shovel like a bird egg which has fallen from a tree. A crumbling jawbone. The bronzed splinters of tiny teeth.

Prudence was right: there is a body buried in my father's grave. But who is it?

CHAPTER 21

Two days after laying Verity in the ground, I slept through my early morning alarm call. I woke up at ten, hungry. I showered and shaved. I didn't want to drink, and more importantly, I enjoyed the process of work. This is what I image a blood transfusion to be like, where every inch of you within feels anew. Every square volume of my old self replaced with a pure, untainted source of contentment. Even my skin has more colour.

Then it all ends with a phone call.

At first there is a long pause, followed by the sound of glass tapping against teeth.

'Hello?' I ask.

The voice is low, brusque.

'Your mother, have you seen her?'

I can hear bristles of an unshaven jaw brushing against the phone's mouthpiece creating a noise like sandpaper rubbing against stone.

For realism, I ask who it is.

'Harry.' he says. 'Have you seen her?'

'How did you get this number?'

'Verity's address book.'

'No, I haven't seen her,' I say.

'Don't lie. Saturday. You came here. You saw her then.'

'I had to cancel, Prudence took ill and she needed me. I rang, to explain.'

Beat.

'She's gone,' he says. 'Took off someplace, fuck-knows-where.'

'Where?' I ask.

'I just said. Why the fuck would I ring if I knew where she was?'

My feet beat a crazy drumbeat to compliment the tapping of

uneasy fingers.

'I talked with your sister. I say talk. She put the phone down on me. What is it with the women in your family?'

It's rhetorical but part of me wants to counter the question by asking what is wrong with all women.

'She's got form for this,' I say instead.

'What'd you mean?'

'I mean, she's done it before. A long time ago. She was seeing this guy, and then for no reason she just upped and left. Is her suitcase gone?'

'And most of her clothes,' he replies.

'Then I doubt she'll be coming back anytime soon.'

'Where did she go?' he asks.

I clear my throat, repeating the same question.

'When she left that other time, where did she go? Maybe I can go and find her?'

I picture Harry in my mind: bloodshot corneas, eyelids purple, cheese string hair sticking to his face, a tumbler filled with bourbon. Poor bastard.

'She had a habit of visiting a retreat, in the woods,' I say. 'Total isolation. A place she could gather her thoughts. She gets like that every now and then. But she never told me the address. That's the point of a retreat; you cut off from society, problems, life.'

'What if you're wrong? I should phone the police. She could be kidnapped, or...'

'Or what? You saying she could be...'

I let the inference hang in the air like a bad smell.

'I'm not thinking straight,' Harry says. 'I don't mean to scare you. But it's best I phone the police, to make sure.'

Fuck.

'There's no need,' I say. 'Give her time. She'll ring you, I'm sure of it.'

'Even so, I should let them know.'

All I can think about is the rug and if he's noticed it missing.

'How silly will you feel when she turns up and you've wasted the police's time?' I ask him.

Beat.

'You think she's on this retreat?' he asks.

'Pretty sure,' I say.

'You think she'll come back?'

'If she doesn't, then she's a fool.'

Applause. Bow. Flowers. Curtain.

A low muffled thud follows a sharp intake of breath. He's finished his drink and placed the tumbler on a table, probably the same table I lunged over to spear a fork in my mother's throat.

'You're right,' he concedes. 'Once I hear back from her, I'll let you know. But if you remember anything about that retreat, a name, even the area, ring me on my mobile and let me know.'

Harry reads out his mobile number and then puts the phone down.

From an outside line I ring Prudence. I tell her what Harry said.

'You did well,' she replies. 'The retreat idea was an excellent improvisation.'

That night sleep fashions a blood-stained hand rising out from my father's grave, grabbing my ankle. In the early hours when my heart is at its weakest, the distress of this vision could be fatal. But nothing happens. No pain. No end. I pay the Sandman for absolution, but instead receive his apathy.

CHAPTER 22

Securing the clasp to the watch around my wrist, Prudence says, 'Your average heart rate is two hundred and twenty, minus your age.'

I do the math in my head.

'It might be best if we take it down by another twenty, just to play it safe.'

Prudence punches the numbers into the watch as I stare down at two perky breasts pressed up tight in a black bra. If I had to guess, my heart rate is already up to two hundred.

'If it beeps, we'll know to stop and wait,' she says.

She kisses my cheek with glossy pink lips and climbs on her bed.

'You like my socks?' she asks rearranging four scatter cushions resting against the headboard.

Two little white Bobby socks, the trim a frilly icing cake design, finish off the ensemble of schoolgirl white shirt, pigtails tied with red ribbon, and denim skirt so short it barely hides her arse cheeks.

Reclining into the bed, one leg leaning over the other to reveal no knickers, she says 'Show it to me.'

I undo my belt, pull down my trousers, and penguin walk over to her. Prudence opens her legs to expose skin so smooth and flawless it reminds me of a Volkswagen Beetle's bonnet.

She notices me looking and says, 'Shaved especially for the occasion.'

I look at my watch: one hundred and twenty bpm.

Two hours previous to this and I'm explaining the nightmare I had about Verity pulling me into the grave. I told her I was worried about Harry, and how sooner or later he will call the police and they'll come to me and ask about this retreat bollocks. Prudence laughed.

"I don't even know if they have such things over here," I said.

And she laughed again and added, "Nothing is permanent in this world, Jack. Not even our troubles."

There's no way Prudence thought that up. I would have asked her where she stole it from, because she probably did, like she stole my heart, but by then she'd already unbuttoned her shirt.

'Smile,' she now says.

A sheet of bright light takes me back to the taxi with the manta-ray eyes and the tattoo of a porn queen.

Blink once, twice. Prudence's hair is bleached, eyebrows and nostrils the same. Blink and she's colourised again.

'I thought it might be good to document the occasion,' she says.

Prudence wants to remember the shirt I'm wearing. The colour of my shoes. She wants to remember my expression before we have sex for the first time: the little things that make the difference.

She grabs my penis and slowly opens her mouth. Absurd thoughts drift in and out of my mind deadening every part of me. I look down and her left arm is held at full length, the camera lens pointing to her profile, her chin pushed down making it look fat.

The shutter opens. Another atomic blast.

With eyes pressed tight, I say, 'The developing laboratory will never let that photo pass. Regulations have to be adhered to otherwise they'll lose their license to trade.'

She mumbles something, the vowels sending small vibrations along the head of my penis.

Pulse is at one hundred and thirty bpm.

Prudence withdraws, stalactites of her spit dripping from my full length. She then guides me inside her like she's performing hari kari. She inhales deeply. Head thrust back. Mouth open wide enough I could perform a root canal.

One hundred and forty bpm.

'My pulse is critical.' I say.

'Just a little longer.'

A wild bull kicks out, rodeo style in my chest. As I drive my pelvis back and forth, I question this need to go through an act that could end up an amusing story paramedics tell their friends. The scene plays with them laughing, telling the nurses and orderlies back at the hospital how they literally had to remove a stiff out of a naked woman.

Prudence gasps. Fingernails dig into my back. She slides her hand down between us and starts to rub one out. I increase the beats of my pelvis. Prudence moans rise and fall like an ocean wave. The watch beeps, and for the briefest of moments, I wonder if today will be the day the medication fails me. She then let's out a cry, something primal that makes veins extend along her neck and her back arch. In that instant her internal muscles tighten around me like a clenched hand. I last only a second longer before falling back on the bed. The ceiling is a foreign sky filled with tiny, little white spots. I look down at my hands: knuckles white, fingernails a dark purple.

The bed shifts and creaks. Prudence's face is where my hand is, cheeks flushed, the ribbons in her hair cascading over her forehead like blood.

'What does the watch say?'

I flip my wrist over and see the numbers, one hundred and ninety five.

'It says I'm fucked.'

The bed creaks again as Prudence withdraws herself from view. I hear the beat of her naked feet on the cool hardwood floor. The bedroom door opening. I undo the watch's clip and throw it into a bowl on the bedside cabinet. The momentum forces it to bounce out and fall to the floor. I reach between the cabinet and the wall. Dust collects on my fingertips. I could never live in a house this dirty. Stretching out farther, my fingers assemble over a foreign surface, its edges bevelled. I tug at its corner, dislodging it from where it's trapped. I pull it out and notice it's an old photo album, dusty and bound in red velvet. This must be the same Prudence told me about. I open the first page and a picture slips out, its back thick with dried yellow glue. It shows a pair of men's shoes, a heavy crease running along the front, sides scuff marked. A flush from the toilet. I place the picture back in the album but not before noticing other pictures, each cello-taped and fixed to black boards: one shows a set of cufflinks, gold, shaped like two diamonds; a pair of muddy pants; a teddy bear. Each image is yellowed and blurry. The creak of a nearby floorboard forces me to shut the album quickly and slip it behind the cabinet again.

When Prudence walks back in she asks how I'm feeling.

'Getting there,' I say.

'You stopped that annoying beeping then'

'Yes, but at the cost of losing the watch. I think it fell behind the cabinet. I've not tried looking yet. I'll get it in a minute, once I've rested.'

'It's okay, I'll do it,' she says moving quickly towards the cabinet.

I sit back and look at the ceiling as Prudence drags the cabinet away from the wall.

'Here silly,' she says handing me the watch.

I apologise.

'Keep it safe. It's not shock proof.'

'Not about the watch,' I say.

'What?'

'I wanted to be there for you, to last the distance. Guess I was afraid something might happen.'

'I enjoyed it,' she says.

Prudence taps the side of my thigh for me to move over. Taking a seat on the edge of bed, she says, 'I think we need to talk.'

'About?'

'Commitment,' she says.

Commitment? I'm taken aback. I thought she would never tender such a word. I say it again in my head: *Commitment*. The need to have sex today was offered under the pretence that my heart condition was mostly in my head. She said it was high time we put her theory to the test. The effort that went into it had me believing it was more than research. Prudence had taken the time to shave herself, dress provocatively. If it was an experiment, she could have fucked me in her dispenser's uniform. Instead, she made an effort. She even documented the whole session with her camera. All this could mean we have moved on an extra step. Now our bodies have engaged it's time for our feelings to do likewise, for me to confirm the love I have felt between us for so long, and she to reciprocate.

'Commitment?' I ask.

'To the inevitable.'

What sickens me more than knowing this has nothing to do with love is the realisation that in the next few minutes we will relive the deaths of all our victims again.

'Haven't you learned anything?' she asks.

'I've learnt things,' I say, hoping my tone is evident enough that I don't want to talk about this right now.

'What have you learnt?'

Lay on the bed with a flaccid penis puts talking about accepting my mortality right at the bottom of the list of priorities. All I want to do is to cover myself up, but Prudence is sat on the edge of the duvet, trapping the sheets.

'All those moments you've spent in its company, and you don't know anything about it yet, do you?' she asks.

I lift myself up by my elbows so my back rests on the headboard. The shift in position allows my crotch to find sanctuary under a loose fold within the duvet, the space large enough to accommodate everything other than my left testicle.

'Are you listening?' asks Prudence. I look up and nod my head. 'Then what did I say?'

'Company.'

She shakes her head.

'Not everyone gets the same privileges as you.'

'Privileges? Death is hardly a privilege.'

'Don't be naive. Think back to those last few moments, each expression, how it changed. Don't you remember?'

I try to move off the bed but Prudence puts her arms out, blocking me.

'You're not leaving until we've talked this out,' she says 'I want you to remember all those faces.'

'Fine,' I say.

'Stop acting like a little child. Remember, for me.'

Light diminishes on the present, its beneficiary the bleak haze of reminiscence. I see a pigeon wing flutter, black peppercorn eyes and the red spatter of blood bleeding into each feather.

'Think how they changed.'

I catch the stench of Mr Sanderson's vomit, and recall the fear of seeing his body shake, giving up, or trying to hold on. The folds of skin on his hands as they clenched tight, nicotine-yellow in the centre, weakening to ivory at the edges. Old photographs: black and white in cheap wooden frames showing the younger Mr Sanderson, the one who served his country, leaning against the long funnel of a cannon. His friends, soldiers, all with the same smooth faces, the same sun in their eyes. The shadow of the photographer cast over each.

'Remember their suffering and how they used it to make sense of their lives.'

Ilse: purple veins navigating through pale hands. Fine elephant hair that covered her upper lip. The smell of Battenburg cake.

'The more they suffered, the more they felt that all the bad mistakes they made in life, all the wrong turns, they were not their doing. It was someone else's fault. A higher force. Fucking God, Ala, Buddha, Ronald McDonald. It's not their fault life turned out the way it did. Bad luck is their motto. We are victims of circumstance their litany. But without misery, without the pain of their suffering, they are empty.'

Miller, the bedraggled furniture and foul stink of his home. A fearful expression, a warped mask bent by years of persecution, of anger and frustration. Eyes, pale and milky, fractured by veins like roots from a tree.

'But the truth is, they were all victims of their own selfishness. They wanted more than the world could offer: to be loved, to be happy, to never be alone. They wanted sympathy, and no one but us gave it them. We gave them respite. We gave them peace.'

Black eyes and lips. The blossoming rose speared by the silver prongs of a fork. Heavy breath mired by blood.

'No more bills to pay, no more voices at the end of the phone selling them health insurance, car warranty cover, home protection policies. No more health problems, no more noise. Everlasting serenity. The ultimate liberation of fear. We gave them this gift. And in return you were given knowledge.'

'What if we're wrong?' I ask. 'What if death is no better than life?'

Prudence kisses my lips, soft and slow. The fetid and sour stench of me still lingers around her mouth.

'Nothing is worse than a life by yourself, Jack,' she says. 'Nothing.'

CHAPTER 23

The television in the hotel room is really a snow globe. The advertisement where the mother micro-blasts a hydrogenated meal for four: a snowstorm churns through the middle of the kitchen.

'We should change rooms,' I say to Prudence.

Flick to another channel: a deodorant advertisement. A man walks through an arid sand dune, the sun beating on his skin, lips cracked and dry. But here, in this shit-hole of a hotel, the desert is as white as Bedford Falls. I hit the side of the TV. Static. I move around the back, and with fingers wiggling the coaxial cable, I ask Prudence if the reception is better.

From the bed she says, 'Can you hear them?'

I return to the edge of the bed and pour myself another whisky. Prudence jumps up and down on the bed. The contents slosh around the glass. I ask her to stop for a second while I pour. She mumbles something I can't hear over the sound of squeaky bedsprings.

When the bed finally comes to rest, I hear more bedsprings squeaking from the room next door. I turn and see Prudence with her ear pressed up against the wall.

'He's really giving it to her,' she says.

I turn back around and finish pouring my drink.

'It's kind of a turn on, don't you think?' she asks.

I don't say anything.

'Think about how many people have had sex on this bed.'

'I'd rather not,' I say.

Prudence resumes jumping again.

'People come here for two reasons: fucking and hiding. Sometimes both. Don't you think that's sexy?'

'No,' I tell her.

I feel Prudence's arms wrap around my chest, her face nuzzled deep in my neck, biting, licking my flesh.

'Girl on girl action? Threesomes? Doesn't that get you hot? To think all that could have happened right here, on this bed?'

'Girl on girl action?' I ask, casually, wondering if this is something Prudence has done in the past.

With a smile I feel pressed to my neck, she whispers, 'It gets me wet.'

I pull her arms away and get up.

'We passed a convenience shop on our way up here,' I say. 'I'll go get us more supplies.'

Prudence lets out a little whimper before falling back on the bed. Stripped to her underwear, two peanut-sized nipples poke up from a white tank top she's wearing. Little skimpy knickers, the cotton in the centre darkened to a dirty grey colour, the elastic around the waist frayed.

Prudence asks, 'Did you bring the heart rate watch?'

Slipping on my shoes, I tell her, 'I'm going to the convenience shop to pick up a bottle of something.'

Her body rolls across the bed, one hand reaching up inside her vest, pulling at the nipple.

'I'll bring back some chocolates, Belgian, because they make the best chocolate.'

She slips her other hand down her knickers.

'I'll knock four times,' I say rapping the door with my knuckles so she can memorise the pace and sound, and she purrs like a cat.

Prudence thought it best we get away for a few days, but not too far we look like we're running away. The change in scenery will do the both of us the world of good, she said. That way I could stop thinking so much about Harry and what he might be doing to try and find Verity. Prudence phoned work and called in sick. I never turned up for work. Desmond has been more lenient regards my attendance. I guess he thinks I'm going through some kind of meltdown or something. Maybe he doesn't even know I'm gone. Maybe, I think, I was never really there to begin with.

I drive about three songs on the radio before finding the shop. Lonely plastic buckets filled with atonement flowers rest against whitewash walls. Next to those sits a display cabinet, its scratched Perspex door protecting the morning's national tabloids from the elements.

I pick some flowers from the bucket and head into the shop.

The man behind the counter is young, good-looking and too busy squeezing a set of handgrips to even look at me. I ask him where he keeps the whiskey, the good stuff, and he raises a finger to the far corner of the store.

'Third aisle,' he says.

A bottle of one-year-old single malt. I find a box containing chocolate shaped into small seashells. Placing all items on the counter, the man stops squeezing his handgrip to say, 'You're dripping.'

The green stems of the flowers are leaking water, blurring newspaper ink stacked on the counter.

'You'll have to pay for that,' he says pulling the top copy away from the rest.

He's big and I don't want to argue. He takes my money and I head back to the car. Inside, I open the bottle of whiskey and take a large swig. It tastes awful but pleases my stomach and head. Screwing the cap back on, I slip the bottle under the seat so it doesn't raise any suspicion should I pull up beside a policeman, a ruse marred only by the bottle being too long to be hidden successfully. Taking the newspaper I was forced to purchase, I lay it on top of the bottle, hiding it completely from view. In doing so, I catch sight of the headline. The ink is smudged but it's still readable. Four words come together, each as fast as a boxer's fist:

Local Woman Feared Kidnapped.

I knock four times on the hotel door but there's no answer. I knock again and check the number to make sure it's the right room. After the fourth time, I enter. The smell of dry cured meats charges the air inside the room. I hear the shower running. I shout to Prudence that I've been outside knocking on the door for over five minutes: a lie, but she doesn't hear me over the water to know this. I find my glass and fill it up again. Prudence walks out of the shower, naked, her hands rubbing a towel through her hair.

I throw the paper on the bed, each page rippled where the heat vents from my car dried it out.

She drapes the towel over a chair and sits on the corner of the bed, reading.

'Oh,' she says.

'Fucking right, Oh.'

I fill my glass again.

'You're not going to start freaking out, are you?' she asks.

I don't answer.

'The police are just doing a few preliminary searches.' she says, reading. 'It seems quite standard.'

'It mentions her name, Verity Glass. It has a quote from Harry. The police could be knocking on my door, right now. Maybe we should head back. It might look suspicious that we've left.'

'But I thought we left so we could spend a couple of days together?'

I hear the faint creak of wood, the rusty springs of another bed beyond the walls.

'I thought this was our time,' she says, and I hear the next-door's headboard hitting our wall.

Prudence is right, people only come to these places to have sex or run away from their problems.

'If the police know I'm here it's going to look like I'm trying to avoid them,' I say.

Half of her is listening to me and the other half seems focused on the wall.

'What should we do?' I ask.

'I think you should cut down on this,' she says taking the glass out of my hands. 'The last thing we need is you being pulled over for a DUI. You need to shower and shave, too. If the police come round to your flat, you'll need to look like you're completely unaware Harry went to them. Better yet...'

Prudence goes over to my overnight bag, knees bending to cup each breast. She rummages through my clothes until she finds my phone.

'Ring them,' she says sitting back on the bed. 'Tell them you've just seen the paper. Sound distraught. Tell them you've been away, with me, an anniversary present. Ask them if it's true that Verity has gone missing, that she's been kidnapped.'

I reach for the glass on the floor.

'No, you need to do this now, with a clear head,' Prudence says, moving it away with her foot.

'My head hasn't been clear for some time.'

A young woman moans from next door, the thud of the headboard getting louder.

'That will add to your performance.'

This is the Second Act. To Prudence, this moment right here is when the plot becomes rich with choice. She knows after this phone call our storyline together will move forward, and from thereon in, there will be no turning back.

'I don't have a number,' I say.

Prudence searches the page until she finds one. She points to it and I begin pressing the digits into my phone. From beyond the wall the woman calls out for Christ.

'Sound confused, distressed,' she says.

'That won't be too hard.'

I get put through to a woman, voice weak, distant, as if she's speaking through a headset. I tell her my name and that I've seen the article in the local paper. She asks me when I last saw my mother.

'A few weeks back,' I say.

Beyond the wall the woman searching for Christ is now encouraging her lover to go faster. On cue, the bed wheezes under the strain of every beat. Part of me knows Prudence, and the things she says, the words and term she uses, it's more than passion. She's heard them before, mimicked from people like the woman beyond the wall, the one who's now offering either orifice to the man.

'We all had dinner,' I tell the operator, 'my girlfriend, Harry, and myself. I can't remember the day.'

The operator says, 'Not to worry.'

'Ask her what you need to do,' whispers Prudence in my ear.

I repeat her words.

Placing my hand over the mouthpiece, I whisper back to Prudence, 'I need to go to my local police station. Today.'

Prudence pouts.

The last thing I say to the operator is how much it'll kill me if anything has happened to my mother.

Prudence is sat on the bed, head pressed up against the wall, listening to the woman reaching an orgasm.

I terminate the call and say to Prudence, 'I best take a shower.'

She keeps staring at the wall, spine nothing more than a string of beads pushed up through pale skin. I'm close enough to see scars, little faint lines scored and raised in the skin. The tip of my finger grazes one, a thin lip running under her shoulder blade.

'What are you doing?' she asks, turning to me.

'How did you get them?'
'What?'
'The scars, on your back.'
'Don't remember,' she says in a whisper.
'There are a lot of them.'
'Really?'
Her fingers causally navigate her back, eyes once again fixed on the wall.
'I've bought you flowers. They're on the side cabinet, near the door.'
She looks over briefly.
'Thanks,' she says turning back. 'That's real sweet of you.'
Next door, the woman finally succumbs to exhaustion.

CHAPTER 24

Detective Tom Nolan carries a brown office folder in his hand and twenty-two pounds of excess fat around his waist, neck speckled red with dried blood. Out-dated moustache.

'Take a seat, Mr Glass,' he says with panda eyes and three-day stubble.

Detective Nolan hasn't been able to manage the work/life balance, opting for long hours at his desk, convenience foods with hydrogenated fats, and blunt razor blades. All of this tells me he's dedicated to his work, which worries me. I look around the room and notice there are only two seats, one table. No plants, no freestanding cabinet finished in walnut, no windows. Just a table, two chairs, a radiator, a large black box with twin cassette decks, CCTV camera in the corner and two fluorescent light strips above us, under which my skin looks translucent.

'You mentioned to the police officer at the desk you've not seen your mother for some time? Do you know how long exactly?'

When Detective Nolan speaks, his breath tells me he's skipped lunch.

'Not sure,' I say. 'Probably a week ago, a little longer maybe.'

'Do you know what day?'

'Must have been a weekend. I work during the week. Have you any leads?'

He opens the folder.

'At this stage we're just questioning the neighbours, family and friends. We like to build up a picture of the events leading up to the disappearance.'

Two fat pubescent girl's breasts press up tight against the sheer cotton of his shirt, and I wonder briefly if Detective Nolan's wife finds man-boobs attractive. Then again, he doesn't look the type to be married.

'You mentioned in a conversation,' he says flicking over a few pages in the folder, 'with a Mr Bryson...'

I question the name.

'Mr Bryson, your mother's boyfriend.'

'Harry?'

'Yes. You mentioned to him your mother may be on a retreat?'

'I did. She's into all that inner harmony baloney. A real earth person.'

'Do you know where this retreat might be?'

'I don't, sorry.'

'No idea at all? A name?'

'No,' I tell him.

'Maybe your sister might know...' He flicks over another page. 'Anne Marie, or maybe your aunt?'

I'm back in the hotel room; Prudence is buttoning up my shirt. She's telling me I'll do fine as long I don't fidget, leave out pronouns, speak excessively in an effort to convince, or use sarcasm or humour to avoid the question. She told me not to look up and to the left because this means I'm visually constructing an image, something that will be construed as a lie, and not to look down too much either, because it lacks sincerity. If I have to look anywhere except the detective's eyes, then look to the right because it signifies I'm remembering an image from memory. Prudence also told me to be concerned to the point of aggravation. I was the one who needed answers, not them.

I tell Detective Nolan I'm scared.

'What will happen if my mother has been kidnapped?'

He closes the folder and leans forward, his chubby white hands resting over each other.

'Try not to worry. We're doing all we can. Most cases, similar to these, are nothing more than a misunderstanding. The person turns up out of the blue. Sometimes people need to get away from everything. I'm sure she'll be back.'

'Why did the papers print she was kidnapped?'

'Mr Bryson is concerned. He told us about the conversation you both had, but he's not convinced she's on a retreat. Why do you think that is, Mr Glass?'

'He's paranoid.'

'Paranoid? Why?'

'My mother has a habit of running away from her problems. She's had a lot of boyfriends since my father died, and well, you know, she's not one for settling.'

'Your mother and Harry were splitting up?'

'No. I don't know. Maybe. I know my mother, and I got the feeling their time had come to an end. I'm guessing Harry knew it too but is refusing to accept it, which is why he can't accept that she needs a little space.'

Detective Nolan eyes me for a moment before saying, 'Did your mother ever feel threatened by Mr Bryson?'

'Threatened? God no. He's a pussycat. Sure, he has a bit of a drinking problem, and my mother does seem a little quiet around him, but he's a big character, you know? He likes to dominate the conversation. Take control. But threaten? No. I can't imagine he'd do anything like that.'

I can almost hear the Detective's cogs turning in his head.

'He tried getting hold of you,' he says. 'Several times, but you've not been at home. He also tried your sister, but I'm led to believe she wasn't very cooperative.'

I nod.

'She doesn't take kindly to be disrespected,' I say.

'Why would you think she was disrespected?'

'Oh. Well, it's just she's quite a reasonable person. The only times I've seen her... how was it you phrased it? Uncooperative? The only times I seen her be like that is when someone disrespects her. You know, like, if they're being a dick and shouting.'

He writes something in a small notepad.

'I'm sure whatever was said, Harry didn't mean it. Like I said, he's a pussycat. But he can come across, if you don't know him very well, a little... intimidating. I'm sure it's the by-product of worrying about my mother. People handle their emotions in different ways. Harry has a shorter fuse than most. But like I say, he's a pussycat. How is he, by the way?'

'He's concerned.'

'Aren't we all?'

The Detective nods and adds, 'He wants her found and he felt the media might be able to speed things along, which is why the local paper ran the article. We did try and persuade him to allow us to conduct our main line of enquires, but he was very insistent.'

'That's Harry. If he cannot get his own way, he takes control of the situation. So what can I do to help?'

'At this stage, there is nothing you can do, Mr Glass. My advice is to go home in case your mother tries to contact you. But if you remember anything about that retreat —'

'Yes, I'll let you know right away.'

He forces a smile revealing crooked teeth.

'Try to remain calm, Mr Glass. We're doing all we can to find your mother.'

I get up and make my way to the door. Before reaching it, he shuffles the papers in his hands and says, 'One final thing before you go…'

I turn around slowly.

'It's probably nothing, but Mr Bryson mentioned something.'

My hand rests on the handle, sweat gathering, the floor beneath me turning soft as hot tarmac.

'The rug, the one in your mother's dining room, it was missing. You wouldn't know anything about that would you?'

I look up and to the left.

CHAPTER 25

Mandrake tells me about a bridge in Peru. Every year the Incas of Huinchiri help rebuild a suspension bridge over a canyon that links two villages. Their ancestors would use the bridge for transporting supplies from village to village.

'This bridge,' says Mandrake, 'could carry the weight of a horse and cart.'

Campbell is sifting through pictures of women. The Internet Company he approached about buying a mail order bride has sent him a handful of possible candidates that fit his budget, though not his taste.

'What about her?' Campbell asks holding up a picture of a woman dressed in black, two front teeth crossing over each other like a Chinese Nosferatu in drag.

Mandrake breaks off from telling me how tradition is the glue to humanity to say, 'She looks untrustworthy.'

Campbell turns the picture to me and I shrug my shoulders.

'She looks nice,' I say.

Wiping his mouth, Mandrake says, 'Nice gets you a birthday card. Nice buys you the polyester and cotton mix socks that let your feet breathe. Nice will not get him laid three times a day.'

On hearing this, Campbell throws the picture in a small waste paper bin behind the bar. After finishing his drink, Mandrake tells me more about the bridge.

'It's hand-woven using qqoya grass. It takes over a hundred individual strands of grass to make up one piece of rope. And the same amount in rope to build the bridge.' He raises his index finger in the air and says, 'One piece of grass. Think about that kid: one strand woven into another, and then another, each one making secure the next. Each strand making stronger the last.'

'What about Mi Ling?' asks Campbell.

We both look at the picture of a woman with red lips and small breasts.

'Notice how her nose turns up at the end?' Mandrake says. 'A sign of laziness.'

Campbell throws the picture on the last.

'Do you understand what I'm telling you, kid?' asks Mandrake.

I rotate a bar mat, corner to corner.

'There isn't anyone on this planet strong enough to be alone. No one. We need people around us to make us stronger. We need people to help take the weight we can't carry.'

'And who do you need?' I ask him.

Smiling, he says, 'Only my shadow.'

Mandrake orders two more drinks and I tell Campbell to add two whisky chasers. Mandrake doesn't protest.

'I'm sure your mother will be fine,' Mandrake says. 'But now you need support from family, and that girl of yours. You need to stop hanging around with us bums.'

Campbell holds up another picture, this time the girl is too thin. Her clothes hang shapeless on a misshaped body. Her nose is huge, bigger than Mandrake's, and one of her eyes looks sleepy. This is all the Mason jar could afford, the rejects, the chaff separated from the wheat.

Mandrake shakes his head and Campbell throws the picture on the other two.

When Campbell's not looking, I lean into Mandrake and ask, 'You think it's true what they say, about how we'll all be judged...when we die?'

'A kid your age shouldn't be thinking like that.'

'I was thinking more about the people who may have kidnapped my mother. Not me.'

Blowing smoke into the lights above the bar, he says, 'Sounded to me like guilt.'

I look at Campbell pulling beer from the pump. Coins dance in an old man's palm waiting to be served. There's no time for me to explain to Mandrake, to unburden myself, least not before Campbell returns. I imagine for a moment that all the guilt and anxiety of killing my mother, and all those other people that's been holding tight my stomach in its fist, is gone. The impish winds that taunt me in the street, the rasp of naked trees sprouting from the graveyard; they no longer overawe me. The grey sky that hangs over my head blisters and shed its skin: a newborn sky, blue and pure in its place. In my mind I plead to Mandrake to listen and make all these things true, to be the ear of the priest who will not answer the knocks at his door. Be the person who will not judge. I know that patience and compassion will help lift the weight I carry, and the slightest hint of sympathy from him will help straighten my back, allowing me to look ahead instead of behind. I know these things because both Mandrake and I are bad apples from the same diseased tree, decayed by the brutality of stoicism. Can you hear me, Mandrake? I want to tell you I'm lost, and that nobody cares to seek me out. Not even Prudence.

Campbell takes the change from the old man and returns to us. Retrieving the pictures he placed behind the optics, he says, 'God knows what I'm gonna do. My budget just doesn't allow straight teeth and big tits.'

Mandrake peers at me through cavernous eyes, a spider web of lines pulling across his forehead. For a second, and from the look on his face, I think he has heard my plea.

Shuffling the pictures, Campbell says, 'Look at her!'

In the picture a woman smiles half-heartedly, one side of her face collapsed by a stroke or some other neurological disorder. I finish my drink then knock the whisky down in one. My head is light. I wish Campbell good luck with his choice and pat Mandrake on the back before heading towards the door.

'You off?' asks Mandrake.

'I have to pack. I'm moving in with my girlfriend for a while until my mother is found.'

'Wise decision,' he says.

Holding up his glass in the air, he says, 'To you kid; the single blade of grass waiting to be woven.'

CHAPTER 26

The light on my answering machine pulsates in time with the pain behind my eye. I trail a dirty finger along each number. Ten messages. I erase them all then yank the phone cable out of the wall.

The musty stench of sour milk in the refrigerator reminds me of how long it's been since I last ate at my flat. On the third shelf the pack of processed beef is dirty grey in colour and gangrenous looking in the middle. I take a glass from the basin and fill it with water. Two aspirin in the cupboard deadens the foul taste of beer on my tongue. I go to the bedroom and open my wardrobe. All my clothes look the same: plain T-shirts, the cotton wearing, bubbling around the collars: shirts have the same thickly stained yellow patch on the armpits, collars wilted. I grab a few pairs of trousers and place them in an overnight bag along with underwear, socks, toiletries, toothbrush and deodorant. I add a razor. Disposable, just in case I get any ideas.

The corners of the living room are dark, as if each one is inhabited by a large Muslim woman dressed in a jilbab. I reach for my bag and hear a knock at the door. Through the small peephole is a face stretched from the centre, blonde hair, a swell of dark roots growing from the centre. I press my eye to the glass and two magpie eyes stare back. Her voice calls out my name, hard and sharp like six-inch nails falling on sheet metal. I move away and rest my forehead against the cool wood of the door.

'I can hear you breathing,' says the woman's voice. 'Open the door. We need to talk.'

A distant roll of thunder grumbles in time with my stomach. It feels like an hour has passed before I undo the Mortis, a further month to turn the handle.

'You look like shit,' says my sister.

I find some coffee in the back of a kitchen cupboard. I don't remember buying it so I have no idea how old it is. I tell this Anne Marie and she says she doesn't want a drink. All she wants is to speak to me about Verity. I tell her I'll go buy some fresh, and she yells at me to sit down. The tone in her voice reminds me so much of Verity it's untrue.

I take a seat on the small armchair in the living room. She sits opposite me on the couch.

Looking at the bag next to me, she says, 'Going someplace?'

'A friend's,' I say. 'I'm staying with them for a while.'

She reaches in a small handbag and pulls out a pen and paper.

'Give me the number,' she says. 'I don't want to lose track of you again.'

'They don't have a phone.'

'Give me your mobile number then.'

'What's the big deal about keeping in touch all of a sudden?'

'Are you serious?'

'Probably,' I say.

'The big deal is our mother's gone missing, and I'm getting it in the ear from the police and that fucking creep, Harry. Did he tell you he's been ringing me?'

I nod.

'Not the most sociable of callers is he? The last one was at three in the morning. He always seems drunk. I've stopped trying to be nice. Now when he rings I tell him to fuck off. Mobile number, please.'

I give it her and she writes it down.

'You look well,' I say.

Putting the pad and pen back into the handbag, she says, 'I'd like to say the same. You've lost a lot of weight.'

'I'm in training to run the marathon this year.'

Outside a sheet of rain hits the window and another deep rumble of thunder moves above us.

'Why don't you open the curtains? Let some light in,' she says.

'I prefer it this way.'

'Are you sick? I've read about people like you. People that live in complete darkness. There's a word for them,' she says.

'Blind?'

'Don't be a dick, Jack.'

She's perched on the end of the couch, one leg crossed over the other, both hands resting on one knee. This is the recommended posture for interviews, comfortable but involved, hands positioned so they don't fidget, eyes engaged so they don't appear nervous. This was how Prudence told me to sit at the police station.

'I went to see the police,' I tell her.

'Good.'

'What did they tell you?'

'That they're doing all they can.'

Above us the neighbour's footsteps press heavy on a wooden floor, each creak sounding like a cork being pulled from a wine bottle. The noise causes the inside of my mouth to ache.

'So when did you last see her?' she asks.

'A few weeks back,' I say. 'We had dinner over at her place, with Harry.'

'So you've met him?'

I nod my head.

'Is he as bad as the rest? Is he worse? He sounds worse.'

'He's not so bad.'

'I'm not really that concerned, about mother. Does that sound bad?' she asks.

I shake my head, half confused, half happy too that I'm not the only one who hated Verity so much.

'She was never really a good mother, was she?'

I don't say anything.

'I can't imagine for one minute she's been kidnapped, like the papers say. That's way too exciting for her. Knowing Verity, she's probably met someone else and is fucking their brains out in some hotel.'

I think back to the hotel room and the couple next door. My skin gooses at the thought it could have been my mother in there.

'I told the police the very same thing,' I say.

'They said you mentioned a retreat? To my knowledge, she's never been on a retreat.'

'Uh? I thought she had.'

Anne Marie leans further back in the couch. Shadows drape and sit uncomfortably between each heavy crease on her skirt as she uncrosses her legs.

'Aunt Caroline rang me,' she says. 'She was asking about you. Figured she didn't need to know we've not spoken in a while.'

'Thanks.'

'The police went to see her. All this talk of kidnapping put the wind up her. She wants you to ring.'

Anne Marie reaches into her bag and pulls out a piece of paper.

'Here's her number.'

I take the paper and put it on the arm of the chair.

'When you have time,' she says and I nod my head.

An unwelcome silence descends. It's so quiet I hear my stomach voice its hunger and Anne Marie's, too. I remember the beef slices in the fridge, the sour milk.

'I heard you got promotion,' I say.

'Promotion?'

'Yeah. Verity said something about a team leader's job?'

'When?'

I pause, remembering how it was the night both Prudence and I buried her in my father's grave.

'At the meal,' I say.

'I've not spoken with Verity for over six months. Probably before you moved out.'

'Really?'

'Look, Jack, my visit today isn't solely about Verity's disappearance. There's something else you need to know.'

I know that whatever it is, I can handle it better with a drink in my hand. It's been over an hour since I was with Mandrake and Campbell. The courage and ambiguity alcohol provides is wearing off and my head is now solid as a tree trunk, and my bravery scared witless by possible family revelations.

'Are you okay?' Anne Marie asks.

I mumble a few ill-formed words under my breath and my sister's expression adopts a soberness reserved for delivering news of a malignant tumour.

'This thing I need to tell you,' she says, 'you might not want to hear it, but I think you have a right to know.'

'This place is far too dreary. Why don't we find a better place to talk? I know a quiet little pub not far from here —'

'You need to hear this in private,' she says, cutting me dead.

'Then get to the point,' I say.

'You still visit Dad's grave?'

'I was there the other day. I saw the flowers you left for his birthday.'

'I didn't leave flowers,' she says. 'I've not been to that grave for years.'

'Really? Then who —'

'This is what I need to speak to you about, Jack. Do you remember anything, about Dad?'

The flutter of pigeon wings tumble around my cochlea, the trail of blood leaching from the boy's shoes flicker in my mind.

'Not enough,' I tell her.

'But you remember something?'

'There was something,' I say. 'It was back at Gran's maisonette. There were these boys and they caught two pigeons. They put them against the wall and kicked them to death. I started crying and Dad came for me. He lifted me high on his shoulders and took me inside.'

'You remember that?' she asks.

I nod my head.

'There were no boys, Jack. It was just you there,' she says.

My body leans forward, almost falling towards her.

'When Verity saw all those feathers and blood on your shoes, she went mental.'

As fast as steam leaving a kettle, blood rushes to my cheeks. Mouth turns dry as salt rock.

'They all thought you were crazy: Gran, Verity, even Aunt Caroline thought you might need help. Verity wanted you to see a specialist. But Dad, he wouldn't have any of it. You said he lifted you up and took you into Gran's place?'

My head feels like it's a ton weight. Somehow I gather enough strength to nod it once.

'It was Verity, not Dad. She came out and saw you there, with those pigeons. You were still kicking their bodies when she pulled you away. You wouldn't calm down, so she slapped you. Dad walked in and hit her back. Then he lifted you up on his shoulders and took you upstairs to the bathroom where he cleaned the blood off your shoes. Jack, you did do some seriously fucked up shit as a kid. It put a real strain on their marriage. I guess that's why she gave you a hard time at home.'

Words fall like broken glass from my mouth.

'Does Verity blame me for our father's death?'

Anne Marie moves out of the shadows and says, 'No. She blames you for him walking out on us.'

#

Anne Marie and I walk in silence, our footsteps the only noise as they press into the loose stone chippings lining our path. I am guided past stone-etched cherubs holding harps; angels with heads bowed respectfully, wings crestfallen, long robes pleated and draped over feet the size of a small child's. I am guided past black polished granite, so clear it reflects our bodies back, white like ghosts.

'It took me some time to find,' she says. 'The first time I came.'

'How many times have you been?'

'Three, maybe four now.' Looking up to the sky she adds, 'It still feels weird.'

The path bends to a large hedge with faultlessly cut edges. Beyond it sits a large tree, trunk twisted like two young lovers holding each other. At its feet, a dozen or so headstones stand upright, all different shades of white and sizes. I follow Anne Marie through each one, stopping finally in front of a large, white marble headstone.

'Aunt Caroline told me,' Anne Marie says bending down. She starts pulling at a few stray weeds collecting at its base. 'She wanted me to talk with Verity again, to make amends. She said Verity needed her family around her.'

I'm half listening to Anne Marie while reading the epitaph on the gravestone. A few words tumble down the smooth polished veneer. It says nothing of my father, only his name and when he died. Unlike the gravestone in the cemetery I visit, this one doesn't lie.

'Fifty-one,' I say quietly.

Anne Marie looks up and nods her head.

'Fifty-one is still so very young, but a lot older than we first thought,' she says.

'You mean what we were told.'

She doesn't reply.

I kneel down beside her.

'I was so angry with her,' she says staring at the gravestone. 'I fucking hated Verity for what she did. Do you remember a guy called Ian? He rode a scooter? I was seeing him for about a year before moving out?'

I shake my head, but quickly remember Verity mentioning his name when we were waiting to eat.

'It's not important. Least it wouldn't have been if I didn't love him. But I did.'

Placing a hand on the corner of the headstone, Anne Marie pulls herself up and straightens out her skirt.

'I told Aunt Caroline what Verity did,' she says.

Anne Marie pauses to reflect before telling me what happened. This interval allows me to observe the details of the headstone more closely. There is nothing much to learn from the epitaph other than the date of my father's death, and that he was loved. It isn't clear from the writing whom by. But someone did. They cared enough to bury him in this idyllic plot where trees resemble lovers and the pathways are laid with limestone chips and not the headstones belonging to the dead. There's no graffiti here, nor callous winds and mistrustful clouds staring down. No bunting flaps incessantly from the limbs of trees that resemble corpses. No stems from dying flowers stoop as if ashamed to be seen in the open. This is as near perfect an eternal resting place as any.

'I told Aunt Caroline everything,' says Anne Marie, pulling me back to the moment. 'Remember when she would babysit us? She was so sweet. She took me in after I left home. I guess she hated Verity too, for what she did to me. I think that's why she told me... about Dad.'

I lick my thumb and wipe a trail of bird shit from the J in his name.

Then I say aloud what Anne Marie couldn't.

'Verity fucked Ian.'

I turn to see Anne Marie's eyes welling. I fill in the gaps.

'So Aunt Caroline was pissed about what Verity put you through, and told you the truth about our father?'

A slight pause before her voice presents itself in softer tones.

'It wasn't your fault, Jack. You mustn't blame yourself for him leaving us. Their marriage was broken, and as much as he loved us, he couldn't cope being around Verity any longer.'

I dig the toe of my shoe in the loose stones beneath me.

'Where did he go?'

'Sadlebourne. Eventually he found someone else. Her name is Rebecca. That's the woman he's been with all these years.'

'Marriages break up all the time, Annie, and parents still keep in contact. But our dad just vanishes off the face of the earth? No phone calls? No birthday cards? You tell me he loved us, but what father just cuts off his kids like that?'

Anne Marie takes my hand. It's soft and reminds me of hot summer days as a child playing in our garden.

'It was Verity's fault. Not his. After he left, she hid us from him.'

'What do you mean, hid us?'

'She moved us out of the house and rented a small terrace near Openshaw. You were very young at the time. She even took us out of school.'

It feels like I've been in a coma for twenty-five years and my sister is telling me all the events that happened while I was under.

'Verity didn't want Dad to find us. Not at first, anyway. Not until she'd convinced us he was dead. That's what she told us. She said he'd had a heart attack and passed away. I was so upset.'

'What about the visits to the grave?'

'It was all for show. She knew that if we believed he was dead, it would make things ten times as hard for him. How can a person come back from the dead, Jack?'

'No. This isn't right. That's not the behaviour of a normal person.'

I stop and wonder if Verity was ever normal, in the conventional sense of the word.

'I'm not making excuses for her,' Anne Marie continued. 'After Dad left, some part of Verity broke and never mended. When she found out he was seeing someone else, to all intent and purposes he was dead in her mind. That's how she coped with him not being there: killing him off gave her the freedom to move on. She just had to make it real enough for us too.'

'But there are death certificates,' I say. 'I found them, hidden in a box within the chimney of Verity's bedroom. It had his name, and when he died. It also had our grandfather's. The dates were all different to the gravestone we used to visit.'

Looking out to the grave, she says, 'I don't know. Aunt Caroline never mentioned anything about death certificates. I guess it's plausible she had them made, forgeries. Maybe it was another way for her to cope; a tangible record that made real his death. Retribution you could say. I don't know.'

'I'm not buying it. They looked too real.'

'Have you ever seen a real death certificate?' she asks.

I shake my head.

'Then how do you know what they look like, Jack? If Verity was willing to buy a plot of land and have a gravestone made, then I'm sure obtaining certificates to add authenticity wouldn't be too big a deal for her, would it?'

'If she did have the gravestone made, why have it etched with one date and the death certificates with another?' I ask.

'You're asking me to understand Verity?'

Inside my stomach aches. I stand up quickly and run behind the bench. Doubled over I vomit into a cast iron bin filled with dead flowers. Tears roll down my cheeks, burning my eyes and scolding my nose. When I join Anne Marie back on the bench she hands me a tissue.

'Better?'

I nod and we sit for a moment in silence. A gentle wind ruffles my hair, the same way a father might brush his hand over his child's hair when they've done something good. And for a moment, I feel him near me. The birdsong abates. In the lull I listen for his voice, just a soft gentle word of reassurance, and if not that, my name. To hear my name said by him would make it all right again. To hear my father's voice would have the same heavenly properties of ambrosia. But in the midst of quietness the wind carries only the scent of carnations and damp earth, and a faint, barely audible sound that is more akin to a happy whistle than a word. I accept it anyway, for a whisper in a world of chaos is a fragile but precious gift.

The birdsong commences again and Anne Marie says, 'Verity used to say to me she'd wished she had two girls. Boys were too much trouble. She tried... to have another.'

'Nothing surprises me.'

'She couldn't. You were ten when she went for an operation.'

'A hysterectomy, I remember.'

I think back to the bandages, the smell, and it brings me back to Miller lying dead in his flat.

'Not by choice,' Anne Marie states. 'The doctors found cysts on her ovaries. Turns out they had to be removed. She was devastated.'

'If she couldn't bond with her existing children, why did she want anymore?'

'Maybe she just wanted to see if it would change her. The strange thing is, something did happen. When she couldn't have any more children, she became obsessed with the ones she had. She always wanted us with her. Never out of sight.'

I'm not buying the over-protected mother angle one bit.

'She told me I would die before I'm thirty, Annie, just like every male in the Glass family.'

'She must have thought you'd stay if you believed you were sick,' she says shaking her head. 'She really is fucked up.'

'She hated me,' I tell her.

'No. She used you,' she says. 'You became everything to her. She couldn't control me, not after what she did with Ian. But Verity didn't want to lose you, too. I should have looked out for you more. You were my little brother and I left you with that witch.'

My arm rests on Anne Marie's shoulder. The closing stage of this warmth display of sibling love is cooled by one question, and taking another tissue from her bag, I dab the tears from my sister's eyes and ask, 'How did our father really die?'

CHAPTER 27

The house sits on a plot of land where no one I know could afford to live. The driveway of white gravel snakes from gates taller than I am on tiptoes, and two stone pillars flank a solid oak door higher and wider than most I've ever entered through. It is a home that makes you believe you're underdressed. It is a home for a king.

The woman who answers my knock is not the woman I was expecting. She has long hair the colour of beach wood, the face of a pink balloon, bright with shiny skin at the cheeks and chin.

'Can I help you?' Rebecca asks.

I clear my throat and say, 'Anne Marie said it would be okay to visit.'

Those driftwood eyes widen, forehead relaxes.

She says, 'You must be Jack?'

She leads to me a rustic farmhouse kitchen filled with pine wood cupboards. Engraved roses and thistles creep around each brass handle on its drawers. Wild herbs spill from a window box overlooking a garden I can't see the end of. Above me, copper pans hang from a stainless steel metal frame like hats of the America Civil War.

'Tea?' Rebecca asks.

I nod my head.

The heels on her shoes strike the ceramic tiles with the same rhythm of Spanish castanets.

'You found it okay then?' she says

'I'm not used to this area.'

'We are tucked away a little.'

'It's really nice,' I say.

'Thank you. When my daughter lived here, and your father was around, the place wasn't so big. Solitude has a way of shrinking a person.'

She pulls open a cupboard door and takes out two teacups.

'You look like him, you know?' she says. 'You have the same eyes.'

It's the first time a comparison has ever been made between my father and me. It renders me mute.

'I'm sorry, Jack. I didn't mean to make you feel uncomfortable.' she says, picking up on my unease.

Pointing towards a large farmhouse table, Rebecca directs me sit down. She joins me and we both sit for a while waiting for the kettle to boil.

'I can't imagine what you must be feeling,' she says. 'Your father would have never wanted this for you. He stayed away for the very same reason.'

'It's been a lot to take in,' I say.

'I can imagine. Your sister was the same.'

Rebecca removes two coasters from the centre of the table and places them both in front of us.

'I just wish your father was here to explain. He would have put it much better than me.'

Steam rumbles from the kettle, the click of its switch bringing Rebecca to her feet.

When back at the counter, pouring, I ask Rebecca if my father ever talked about us.

'He did,' she says straining a teabag on the side of the cup. 'All the time. It hurt him that he couldn't be there. But your mother was too shrewd an adversary.'

'You said he stayed away, why?'

'The welfare of his children was your father's main priority, you must understand that. After Verity took you and Anne Marie away, he visited everyone in the family, travelled to every place he and Verity had visited. When he couldn't find you, the police were informed.'

'How long was it?'

'Before Verity returned back home? I don't know, a few weeks perhaps. The police rang your father at work. They told him Verity had reported to the station. Your father wanted the police to charge her and Social Services to get involved. But Verity had that charm about her and explained it as a misunderstanding. She told the police she had taken the children on holiday to avoid any further stress. Blamed your father, saying he was a violent man and she didn't want him near you both.'

Rebecca joins me back at the table and places a China cup down on my coaster.

'A week later she paid us a visit and told us what she did, about faking his death. He almost killed her. It was awful. I'm sure you can imagine how your father felt?'

I nod and take a sip of tea.

Placing her cup down, Rebecca says, 'I'm rushing ahead, aren't I? Tell me something about you, Jack. What is it you do?'

Lately, euthanasia.

'If it's okay, I'd like to know more about my father.'

Rebecca acknowledges my appeal compassionately and says, 'I'd be the very same.'

I prompt her with a question.

'Is it true he was never happy with Verity?'

'No. He did love her, once, but after they married, and Anne Marie was born, something changed between them. She changed. I'm not sure why, exactly. He never went into the details. But your father became deeply unhappy. After he left, your mother was hurt, confused and angry. But the decision to leave your mother was made way before we got together.'

The need to proclaim her own innocence in all this comes as much as a surprise to her as it does me.

'This is quite hard for me to talk about,' she says, as if trying to qualify her discomfiture.

I force a smile, which she seems to like.

'I can see so much of him in you. You both share the same – and I hope you don't take this the wrong way – sadness.'

Placing my cup down, I ask, 'Why didn't he file for custody?'

'He wanted to,' she says, 'but Verity had buried him and took you both to that fake grave. She made his death appear as real as possible. She made it impossible for him to return. If he tried to make contact, the shock of you and Anne Marie seeing him would be too traumatic. And even if he did, and Social Services were called in, your mother may have ended up losing the two things that have kept her alive throughout the break up.' Putting down the cup and tracing her finger around its edge, she adds, 'Losing you both would have meant the end for Verity. Jack, you must understand that your father loved you both dearly, and it tore him in half what she did, but he felt sorry for your mother. In time, a pact was made. Joseph was never to make direct contact, and for that your mother would tell him of places she would take you both. He would have to keep his distance, and there could be no contact whatsoever, but he could watch you grow.'

'He saw me?'

'He's been with you all this time, Jack. He saw you leave school, get a job, rent a place of your own. He's watched you tend to his grave and mourn his death, too. In your heart you may have been searching for him most of your life, but there have been times when he's been only a few feet away.'

An invisible hand grabs my throat.

A Welsh dresser beside me holds a few stray bottles of whisky. Rebecca sees me looking and asks if I would like something stronger than tea. I thank her and she pulls a glass from the shelf below.

'This okay?' she asks lifting the bottle.

Single malt, ten-years maturing. I agree and she pours me a drink.

'Did you marry him?' I ask.

'We'd both been married before and felt it wouldn't be right. But we loved each other very much.'

I pick up my glass. After a few sips, I say 'I went to the grave yesterday. The real one. I need to know, did my father die of a heart attack?'

'He had angina. But it was managed by medicine. Your father was never a slave to his weaknesses.'

'So, if it wasn't a heart attack?'

The reflection of what her mind could see caused her face to pinch together, as if shielding the awful memory of that moment.

'He was walking back from the shop and was knocked over by a car. An off-duty policeman of all people. As it turned out, the officer was drunk. He never even saw your father.'

I hear myself say sorry, as if the man we're talking about is an acquaintance at best, like when you hear a neighbour is dying of cancer, or a teacher you once liked at school. Then I realise he's my father, someone who I've never met, yet within a small fraction of time have learned to appreciate, understand, grown near and lose to a drunken policeman.

'He would have been so proud of you,' she says. 'It's such a shame you both never got to talk.'

Silence is born. During its brief existence all moments with Verity are repeated: the visits to the grave and the guilt she placed on us when we refused to go because it was raining or snowing. The casualties of my fear and distraction, each one helping me come to terms with fate; each life sacrificed because of a lie. My mother was allowed to keep close the only people in the world she had left, her children, the ones she told their father had died, and in return my father became a shadow, a stranger who I may have passed on the street every day.

'Would you like another drink?' she asks looking at my glass.

I agree.

When she's finished pouring, I ask about her daughter.

'I was married before I met your father. This is going to sound like I'm jinxed, but there was an accident and my husband died when she was only young.'

I hear myself say sorry again. She tenders a smile to let me know I didn't need to.

'It was a long time ago.' she says. 'Seems like someone else's life, not mine. You don't fall in love so easily the second time around. But your father had a way about him. He made me feel special again. In time, both he and Felicity became very close too. That's my daughter's name. She was devastated when Frank, her father, died. It took her years to even smile. Joseph never gave up on her though. Eventually she warmed to him. That was the kind of man he was.' Trying to lighten the mood, she adds, 'I hear it's your birthday coming up.'

'A couple of weeks. It was meant to be a big day, but now it'll be much the same as any other.'

'I'm sorry to hear that,' she says.

'No, I'm happy. Normality is the best present I will receive this year.'

I stay for one more drink, after which Rebecca tells me we should keep in touch. She suggests I come round on my birthday. She writes down the home phone number and tells me to ring before I arrive next so she can get a few of my father's possessions together. Then, as if jolted by this reflection, she rushes to the Welsh dresser and begins rummaging through its drawer. A few seconds later she hands me a picture and tells me it was taken a year before he died.

'He loved fishing,' she said.

I look at the picture for a moment. My father is sat beside a small river, hair thin, grey around the temples, deep lines run across his forehead. He has a strong neck, tanned red by the sun, arms that seem at ease holding aloft a silver and green fish. I note familiarity, but not one recognisable to me at first. It's only during the taxi journey back to Prudence's flat I realise it's the same I see in the mirror every day. Rebecca was right. We did look alike.

CHAPTER 28

I hold out the picture of my father to Prudence. She doesn't take it. She just looks at it once, a fleeting glance, and then takes off her coat.

'Don't you want to know who he is?' I ask.

She shrugs and opens the fridge. I slam it shut, nearly taking off her fingers. She walks out towards the bathroom, slamming the door behind her. I try the handle. The bathroom is locked. From behind the door water is being drawn into the bathtub. I rattle the handle and beat my fist against the veneer like some crazy psycho from a horror movie.

'Let me in!'

Silence.

I rest my forehead on the door and say, 'The photo's of my father. Are you not interested? Don't you care?'

Niagara Falls.

'Christ, Prudence! This is something really important to me and you're having a fucking bath?'

I go to the kitchen and retrieve a box of matches and a packet of cotton wool pieces used to remove makeup. I return to the bathroom door.

'If you don't come out in the next ten seconds, I'll smoke you out!'

I start to count.

'One... two...three... four...'

The toilet flushes.

'...six....seven...eight...'

I strike the match and hold the naked flame to the cotton. It goes up kindling. With urgency, I force it through the small gap in the door. Save for the running water, I hear nothing from the other side. I light another cotton ball, and another, all of them burning the tips of my fingers as I push them through the small gap.

'Stop it!' shouts Prudence, finally. 'You're burning the fucking carpet!'

I shout through the gap, 'I'm going to turn the gas taps on!'

I exaggerate every step as if walking away. A few seconds later Prudence opens the door and walks out, eyes red. When I see she's crying, I forget how angry I am.

'You've burnt the carpet,' she says. 'If the landlord sees this I'll lose my bond.'

I look down to see a small black circle where the fabric caught light.

'It's nothing,' I say.

She starts to whimper.

'Jesus, really? You're that upset about a carpet?!'

'It's not that,' she says wiping her eyes.

'Then what is it?'

Prudence says nothing.

I reach into my back pocket and pull out my father's photo.

'This is him, Prudence. This is my father. And he didn't die before he was thirty. He was fifty-one. He died five years ago, run over by an off-duty police officer. The grave we buried Verity in, the skull we found that night, it wasn't his. I've seen his grave. I even met the woman who he loved, the woman who really buried him. Her name is Rebecca. She lives in a big house on an expensive road. She's really nice, Prudence. You'd like her a lot. She told me everything, about my father, why he left us and why he couldn't return, about what kind of man he was, and she told me about Verity. My mother put them both through hell, and yet she always tried to justify Verity's actions to me, as if she didn't want me to think too badly of her. Verity was ill, just not like you said. She was hurting from the break up, insecure, and afraid she'd lose her children. She made it look like he died, because to her, he had. She bought a plot of land and had a headstone made. Anne Marie believes the death certificates I found were fake, made up to convince me I would die when I turned thirty. It was just a ruse to keep me close to her. Oh yeah, my sister came to visit me. We had a long talk too. Seems I was pretty fucked up when I was a kid.'

I hold out the picture a little farther.

'He's a good-looking man, don't you think?'

Prudence is still looking at the carpet burn. With her head low, I can't even tell if she's crying anymore.

'Rebecca said I reminded her of him. I have the same eyes, she said. Do you think I have the same eyes?'

Prudence shrugs without even looking.

I place the photo back into my pocket and put my hand on her shoulder.

'What is it?' I ask her. 'Why are you so upset? Don't you realise what all this means? There is no family time bomb ticking in my chest. Rebecca said my father had angina, but beside that he lived a normal life. I may have inherited a weaker heart than most, but I'm not going to die before I reach thirty. Isn't that good?'

Prudence's eyes are glass, reflecting back all the light in the room.

'I'm happy for you,' she says.

'You don't look it.'

'I feel... I don't know, surplus to requirements now. I don't see how I fit into things anymore? You'll never need another Ilse or Mr Ripley now.'

'No,' I say. 'We can stop the killing.'

'And this Rebecca, you'll probably want to spend more time with her, getting to know your father?'

I shrug.

'So where does this leave me?' she asks.

Wrapping my arms around Prudence, I say, 'We can start being a normal couple. We can make plans and go on holidays, maybe even get a place together. We can plan a future, one I didn't, or couldn't, envisage happening until the last few days. But yes, I will need to find out more from Rebecca about my father, but that won't affect our relationship.'

'You promise?' she asks my shoulder.

'Of course,' I say. 'This is the beginning for us, not the end.'

Prudence undresses and she slips under the bed sheets, naked. No hair ribbons, no kinky outfit, no dirty talk. In the end death did not bring us together, but a common need to feel wanted. In my search to what exists beyond life, Prudence and I were united by the same fears as our victims; we suffered because it made sense to. Prudence once said we are more dead being alive without ever experiencing pain, and for her that may have been true. But I see now she was scared to live a life free from pain, scared to allow herself to be exposed to love. And with every soft stroke and whispered word, every heavy breath and groan of pleasure we both share in this bed, I know she no longer fears this anymore.

CHAPTER 29

Desmond watches me with a keen eye. He's concerned I'm not up for the job. I find him looking out from his office window to make sure I'm keeping up with the orders. It's been three days since I met Rebecca, and three days of sobriety. I still see Mandrake and Campbell most afternoons, and while my abstinence was cause for concern, and especially cruel to Campbell's Mason jar, I have pacified them that my reason for keep a clear head is only while I get my shit together. I then return to Prudence's flat where I wait until she finishes her shift; me, the domestic husband, the person who cleans up her mess and prepares her meals. For three days I have tasted the life of a normal man, engaged in the humdrum acts that would seem boring to most, waltzing each around my head, the wind from their tails clearing the uncertainties resting there. I don't visit the hospital anymore.

Desmond knows none of this.

I look over to his office and he's talking to Mick. They're looking at pages of orders. Before Desmond has time to notice me looking, I turn back to my desk. Tacked on the edge of the Grading table is a yellow note. It tells me to ring Anne Marie. I had two messages from her on my mobile phone telling me a detective Tom Nolan called asking where I am. He's called at my flat several times, wanting to ask more questions. He wants to know if I've heard from Harry. This little yellow note is the same as blood coughed up by the tuberculoses patient, or the violent headaches spawned from a brain tumour. This little yellow note is reminding me there's still something wrong and that things are far from normal.

The chain of linked photographs travel past like a locomotive of memories. Reducing the speed, I see a child opening Christmas presents beside a huge tree. A dog holding between its teeth a wet stick. A sideways glance towards the offices tells me Desmond is still looking so I push the lever back up again.

Lunch is a stale tuna sandwich from the vending machine. In the toilet, I have a great shit and hear myself whistling a merry tune as I wipe my arse. Back on the floor everyone is skating around each other, doing their job.

Work is constant. Nothing changes.

Roll #341 is fed across from one end of the Grading desk to the empty collection spool at the other. Images flash by in a blur. No pinks, no cerise, no flesh. Another spool: #342. No erections, no penetration, no perverse acts of self gratification. The final spool: #345. Streams of colours cut my grading desk in two. My mind drifts away to thoughts of what I can make Prudence and myself for tea. Produce is more of a concern now than death. Where before I would need to memorise the prescribed amount of a Lithium overdose, I now worry about measured quantities of food, and if there is enough at home to make a chilli or pot roast. And like a driver who has travelled twenty miles without taking in a single minute of the car journey, the spool of photographs before comes to an end.

'Fuck,' I say quietly.

I stop the motor and put it into reverse just in case I missed a huge cock. As it makes its slow journey backwards, I catch glimpse of a tattoo, black writing. The word Leviticus, and the numbers 19:28 float around my head.

Nearing the start of the roll again, I stop the motor at a pretty girl eating candyfloss. Lever is switched, direction changed to forward. A slow moving succession of images sees the girl on holiday where a castle sits on the edge of a harbour. I notch up the speed and there's a man waterskiing, children in life vests sat on a boat. One of them is crying. The motor gathers pace again.

Leviticus.

I switch the lever down, slower now. A lake. A duck taking flight. I move from the desk and check the roll number against all the rest I have graded, making sure there's not a copy in the order. No other roll number matches this. I take my seat again and roll the photographs back slowly.

Stop.

Spreading the full width of the desk, four pictures are chained together. The end photo is of a duck taking flight. The one before is a blurry image of a young man hiding his eyes, cobwebs of smoke caught in his hair. Proceeding this is a white light floating, a flash reflection in a window. The final one is a cyclist waiting at a set of traffic lights. I pull the lever to the slowest setting and crawling past me is the arm of the taxi driver who took Prudence and me to Verity's. Leviticus. 19:28.

Panic shadows my face. Everyone around me is busy, skating, cutting, packaging. I flick the lever up and the images move forward once again. The brown flannel I use for my headaches is linked to the suit I wore when I was Mr Price and Mr Alderman. A blurry image of my CDs. The television from the hotel room. A newspaper with words about a kidnapping.

The little things that make the difference.

I reverse the motor to the very start of this batch, to the beginning of my schooling in death: a photo of three soldiers standing next to a cannon. Saliva clatters at the back of my throat like a canopy caught in a storm. I cough a little but no one notices. Another photo, this time of capsules lay strewn next to a bottle of Atenolol, the cap twisted off. A perfectly framed picture of Battenburg cake is connected to a picture of moccasins, a crucifix nailed to a wall, a bottle of brandy. Next is a black stove, fire seen through a small square door, a broken coffee mug tainted red and paintbrush handles submerged in turpentine. I go to the very end of the batch where the last set of pictures shows Prudence's cheek bulging, skin and eyes blurred. An electronic date is printed in the bottom corner, burnt orange, a visual diary of our liberating the sick and the lonely. I dry heave and place my hand over my mouth. A quick glance to the offices and I see Desmond sitting at his desk again, busy at his computer. Unhooking the roll, I take it to a Cutter sat across from me.

The Cutter is wearing headphones, the type that fit in the ear like a doctor's stethoscope. I nudge him. Startled, he pulls one of the headphones away from his ear.

'What?'

I feign a smile and ask, 'What you listening to?'

'What? What do you want?'

'I have a friend who sent some pictures to be developed.' I lift the roll up for him. 'I was wondering... actually, hoping, if you'd help me out and cut the pictures so I can get the batch number and pick them up for her?'

'What for?'

His hostility makes me uncomfortable.

'They're for a friend. I can pick them up so she doesn't need to pick them up herself.'

'We're not supposed to do that,' he says placing the headphone back in his ear.

Grabbing his hand I tell him, 'Okay, it's not really a friend. They're for a girl, an old flame. To be honest, we hardly speak anymore because her boyfriend is the over-protective type. You understand, right? I'm sure you do. I'm not into breaking up relationships, but this guy she's seeing is a real arsehole. I know she'd be better off without him, and she knows this too. But she's scared. The prick has taken away all her self-confidence. I know if I could get her alone for a few hours, well, I'd be able to convince her to move out. But it's having that excuse to approach her. I may have conviction, but I lack originality, you understand? You do understand, don't you? Of course you do. I need something to initiate a conversation. These pictures I hold in my hand could be that conversation. And if there's anything I could do in return, then you only need to ask.'

'You can let go of my fucking hand for starters,' he says.

I do and he inserts the roll into a big machine.

'Give me ten minutes.'

I thank him. Not to raise suspicion I return to my desk and wait for him to finish. My mind freewheels to all those pictures shackled together, each one a splinter from my own memory, chipped away and seen through the eyes of Prudence. The slippers, the hand, they bring me to the priest sat in the kitchen, the sound of wood snapping as it burns in the stove keeping him warm. I remember his kind face, his words. He was the first person to hear me, to cast aside his own concerns to listen to mine. The old woman at the church told me he had taken ill and I was too selfish to pursue his well-being, to see if he was getting better, or worse. The poor priest, a selfless man who asked little of me but honesty, now the victim of what? Jealousy? But how did Prudence know I had spoken with him? What possible threat could he be, a man dedicated to the cloth, discretion and secrecy two guiding principles. What possible gain can be made from his death?

I can hardly see, my eyes filling with tears. I wipe my sleeve over them and notice Desmond looking at me, his forehead dipping in the middle. A second or two later, I hear a voice.

'You must really like her, eh?' asks the Cutter.

He must think my tears are for the girl. I agree and he hands me a cardboard wallet.

Before he leaves, he says, 'Good luck.'

I inspect the contents and find all pictures intact, except those showing my cock in Prudence's mouth. The Cutter must have edited them out. I'm not overly concerned. My face was hidden. I check the pictures once more. Towards the back of the wallet is a new photo showing a pair of black motorcycle boots. The boots are angled is a strange way, with the toe facing at a right angle. The owner had to be lying down when the picture was taken. I try desperately to remember if I've seen those boots, or know who owns them, but no recollection is made other than a reminder, a simple jog of memory that leads me back to the yellow note pinned to my desk.

Before being dispatched, all pictures go to an area of the factory for sorting. The batch number, the same one on the roll, is married together with the personal details of the customer. In the eventuality we stumble on child pornography, pictures of rape, murder, or anything else deemed illegal, illicit or immoral, we can trace the owner and report them to the relevant authority. In the sorting depot, a maze of metal shelving hides me from the other employees, all of whom are dressed in lab coats. I trace my finger over the small white stickers on each shelf, looking for the numbers that match the one on the wallet, the same that will confirm the name and address of the person who took them. Every white sticker looks the same, each slowly blurring into the other. My fingers fall to a sticker with numbers printed on that sound like those I hear in my head. On the shelf, directly above this sticker, is a blue plastic tray. Removing it from the shelf, I look left and right before reading the numbers penned on in marker ink. The numbers tally but the address printed on the order sheet is different. I read the name a couple of times, and it's then I realise the importance of distraction.

It's then I realise Prudence's motives.

CHAPTER 30

The door to the rectory remains mute. I strike it again but little is gained other than a sore hand. In the church a few pious figures sit, backs arched, heads resting on the pew in front. There's a cough from above me. I crane my neck and see a man dressed in a white cassock on a mezzanine floor.

The man in the white cassock is not the priest who sat and listened patiently to me. He is much younger and wears glasses. When he sees me walking towards him, he looks shaken and stops what he's doing.

'Mass is not for another hour,' he says.

Behind him is a large organ, pipes stretching out to the church ceiling like tin soldiers.

'This area is only for the choir,' he says, a tremble now evident in his voice.

Sitting down on one of the chairs, I tell the priest how I wish to speak to Father Branigan.

'I've been trying for a few weeks to contact him,' I say, 'but nobody ever answers at the rectory.'

'You've not heard?'

I shake my head.

'The father died just over a week ago.'

The shock is diluted, thinned out by the pictures that rest in my coat pocket.

I ask him how and a whisper of hesitation crawls over his face.

'Did you know the Father well?' he asks.

'Not really. He helped me out of a bad spell.'

He recommences placing hymnbooks back on each seat, as if to signify his confidence in what I'm saying.

'I understand,' he says. 'The passing of Father Branigan was a shock to us all. I assume you did not attend the mass where we made known his passing?'

I shake my head again.

'Not to worry. Such a small community we assumed it best his congregation not presuppose anything untoward had happened.'

This brings a faint dourness to his expression. I remain fixed with the same expression I left work with, one of fear and anxiety.

'All who attended were told the reason,' he says pushing his glasses to the bridge of his nose.

'That being?'

'Insulin, or lack thereof,' he says.

Hurried images flood my mind of Prudence arriving at the church, talking with the priest, winning his trust. She must have followed me one day when I came to visit. It hits me square across the jaw: the morning she didn't arrive for work and I got in the fight with the fat woman's husband, she must have seen me leave the rectory. He posed too much of a threat to her. People confess all kinds of things to priests. They speak of infidelity, self-doubt, their angers and troubles, things they hope God will absolve. Prudence feared I'd do the same. She was protecting herself, her real identity.

'Are you okay?' asks the priest.

I nod and tell him, 'It's been a busy day.'

He nods and continues with his work.

'Because it never really affected his work,' he says, 'Father Branigan felt it unnecessary for his congregation to concern themselves with his health, especially when he spent so much time doing the same for others.' He turns to me and says, 'It was a peaceful passing. He slipped into a coma and never returned.'

I see black boots in my head.

'If you wish to pay your respects, he is buried in the church grounds.'

I thank him for his time. Making my way down the stairs I hear the priest's voice float over my head, the acoustics lifting it high to the rafters, 'You can't miss it for all the flowers,' he says.

The grave I kneel before has no flowers, the earth sinking once more due to gravity and rain. How many years it will take before the grave sinks to the depth Prudence and I found it that cold night is unknown, but I assume it will be many more than I will see.

It is strange to think that both Anne Marie and I have walked this graveyard for many years while Verity knew it was empty. If I remember her face now, the pain and sorrow in her eyes, the way she would hold both our hands and cry, talking to the sodden ground the way a wife talks to her husband after he returns from work, I feel great sadness. Verity suffered loss. She grieved this loss, and made us grieve it, and in doing so built the memory of a dead but loving father. This was much more romantic than simple defeat: Verity made us love a man we knew nothing of. These past few weeks I have felt my life coming to an end. Each second that passed, my body prepared itself for its demise; muscles weakening as if knowing their services will not be called upon again, bones aching as if anticipating the slow journey of corrosion. Even my eyes began their slow decline into indifference. All this should have changed once the truth was exposed, but instead I feel similar pangs of bleakness. The truth is I will never rid myself from all the death in my life. I will grieve for each, from Mr Sanderson to the priest. But most of all, I will wonder if I was wrong about Verity too.

'I'm sorry, mother. There are no excuses for what I did. I'm exhausted and my heart is weaker for it. And although you made me believe it was much weaker, I know now you did it because you never wanted to be alone. You never wanted to lose the son given by a man you loved. Because of this you did see more than a son. In my face lay echoes of him, of Joseph, your husband, and me, forever the reminder of a life you once had. But I forgive you. And I'm sorry for thinking the way I did. I'll visit soon and bring flowers. I'll clean this headstone and tend to the grass once it begins to grow in spring. I'll pull weeds and cover birthday cards in plastic so the ink does not run in the rain. I will visit until I cannot visit anymore. But if I'm correct, you shouldn't be alone for long. You will have company in this grave soon. Near to you will be a man who loved you very much, more than my father ever could.'

CHAPTER 31

I look through the window into Verity's house. On the dining room table is a bottle of JD and a plate of rotten food. I go around the back of the house to the kitchen window. I clench my hand into a fist and rub out a peephole in the dirt: all the kitchen work surfaces are festooned with take-out cartons. The silver knife I sliced my flesh with is decorated red again, only now with pizza topping. White net curtains make the job of looking through the living room window no easier than the kitchen. I squint, allowing my eyes to readjust to the poor lighting. Eventually I see them, the same black boots I saw in the picture. A body laid limp, arm stretched out. Skin more yellow than pink. Caramel coloured. Harry is dead.

Less than hour later and I'm using the spare set of keys to enter Prudence's flat. They turn within the lock, the door opens, and all at one I'm met by the whispers of Prudence's perfume lingering in the lobby. From behind the bedside cabinet, I pull out the photo album I found after Prudence and I had sex. Pictures present themselves in varying size and quality. It's like being at work again. Only this time I'm not looking for flesh. This time I'm looking for clues. Aged snapshots showing cuff links and dirty boots are framed in a small, square border with eggshell finish. I turn one over and check for a date, but there is no inscription, nothing to indicate when they were taken, or by whom. A few boards in and the quality improves, the pictures enlarged to the standard 6 x 4 ratio. There are pictures of toy ponies with bright pink manes, dolls with eyes missing. A Christmas tree: the branches, naked.

The little things that make the difference.

I turn over and find a photo of a garden shovel, thick with dirt and clay, similar to the one we used to dig my mother's grave. The rest of the photos are of jumpers with bright patterns. Shirts with wide collars. Kipper ties. A sunset. A frozen lake. Snow coating a pretty barnyard. A face, blurred. The black shadow of a moustache. Towards the end of the album is a photo of a plastic hospital wristband. Bringing it towards my face, I can just make out the name: Joseph Glass.

The last four pages remain blank, awaiting new tenants, and all at once I feel the cardboard wallet in my coat pocket that contains the photos I extracted from work. All of Prudence's transgressions, the record of every kill we made and sad victim we committed to the ground, their place destined to be this album. Memories to be preserved.

CHAPTER 32

Rebecca asks how I am.

'Fine,' I say.

I'm not sure she believes this because my voice is weak by the day's discoveries. She doesn't question me, nor push for an explanation. Instead, she sounds genuinely pleased to hear from me.

'I was thinking about you today,' she says.

Prudence's telephone line sends out a crackle of static, prompting Rebecca to ask if I'm still there.

I look at my watch, fearful of the time slipping away, bringing closer the end of Prudence's shift at the hospital.

'I'm here,' I tell her.

'There was a lovely chocolate cake in a shop window I passed on the high street. I thought it would make a wonderful birthday cake for you. But I didn't buy it because I wasn't too sure if you like chocolate. Do you? Like Chocolate?'

I want to tell her how sweet things don't agree with me, but it's such a nice gesture that I agree.

'I am pleased,' she says. 'I did buy it. I didn't want you to feel like you had to eat it just because I bought it especially.' She laughs a little and says, 'I'll buy some candles this afternoon.'

Rebecca seems genuinely excited to share this moment with me, the way I always wanted Verity to sound during birthdays and Christmas. The way a mother should be toward her child.

I call her name softly, the way I would if caught in a dream, and she responds just as tenderly.

'What is it, Jack?'

'My birthday,' I say, 'I might not be able to make a visit.'

'Are you okay?'

I feel myself fold over, doubled up with remorse.

'I'm fine,' I tell her.

'You have other plans?'

'Something like that,' I say.

'Couldn't you come after whatever it is you have to do?'

'I'm not sure.'

'It would make me happy if I could see you. I have some of your father's things.'

I drop to the floor, head resting on the cool kitchen linoleum. When I don't speak, Rebecca asks if I'm okay.

'I'm okay,' I tell her.

'You'll try then?' she asks.

I agree.

I stand and blood rushes to my head. For a few seconds reality and deception blur and I'm lost between the two worlds, unsure if I'm real or dead. Carrying me to the conclusion I'm neither, but misplaced among the hopeless souls destined to never find peace, her voice calls out from the other end of the phone.

'Are you still there?'

'Yes,' I say.

'Is there something you want to ask me?'

'There is something. Your daughter, Felicity...'

'Yes.'

'Did she ever meet Verity?'

'Felicity?'

'Do you remember a time when Felicity talked with Verity?'

'No. Your father and I made an effort to keep them apart. Actually, there was one time.'

'What happened?'

'It was a couple of years before your father passed away. Verity turned up out of the blue. Your father answered. I was in the kitchen but I could hear them arguing on the doorstep. She was demanding money, said he owed her back-dated child maintenance. She was drunk. Your father provided Verity with money whilst you and Anne Marie were growing up, so what she was saying wasn't true. He tried to calm her but she was insistent. He threw some money at her and told her to leave. I don't think it had anything to do with the money. She just wanted to cause your father more distress. Verity finally left and when he came back into the house, Felicity was in the hall. She'd been watching it all from her bedroom window. Joseph tried to convince her that he didn't know Verity, but she heard some of the things that were said, about you and Anne Marie and how Verity wished he was dead. That night we told Felicity everything. She was young, but she always had a maturity beyond her years. Why do you ask, Jack?'

I want to tell Rebecca that the night Verity came to the house became the catalyst to everything; lies, subterfuge, euthanasia, murder. Yes, her daughter did change that night. She became colder, capable of turning off emotion to serve her revenge, and in doing so became a different person with a different name. Every waking moment thereafter she spent learning about medication and the art of distraction. But for Rebecca to know Felicity's aim all along was to get closer to Verity through me would be good for no one. I am just as bad as Felicity, because we wanted the same thing.

'I was just concerned.' I say. 'Verity had a way of sucking people into her misery. It'd upset me to know it happened to your daughter too.'

Rebecca says nothing, which means she too noticed the change.

'I need to know one other thing,' I say.

'Okay.'

'What did your husband do?'

'I don't understand?' she says.

'For a job, what did he do?'

She pauses before answering.

'He owned a funeral home.'

CHAPTER 33

Today there is no Campbell. Instead, Campbell's sister, Pam, is working behind the bar while Campbell goes to pick up his new wife from the airport. Pam has the build of a woman playing ignorant to any nutritional advice: her face is etched with a patina of fine lines only misery imparts. In the short time I have known her, which is half an hour at best, it strikes me Mandrake is quite smitten with her. So much so he seems reluctant to move when I ask him if he'd come and sit with me for a while.

'Never heard the saying, if you stay in one place long enough you'll see the world pass you by?' he asks. 'Well, what if I move and miss the world? With such a busy schedule, do you really think it'll hang around long enough for good old Mandrake?' His lips, cracked and grey, pull wide to exhibit a few black teeth. 'Do you think the world gives two shits about stopping and bearing all to these tired eyes?'

By now Mandrake has Pam laughing, her hand slapping his arm in playful reproach.

'Leave the boy alone,' she says.

'He knows I'm only pulling his chain, isn't that right, kid?' he asks.

I agree, but without clarification I wouldn't have been entirely sure.

Mandrake drops his act long enough to see the seriousness in my request. Throwing a quick glance to Pam, one that tells her he is somewhat duty bound to share time with me, he makes his way over to a small table at the far end of the pub.

'What's the problem?' he asks sitting down, the move making him wince a little.

'I need your help,' I say, and without deliberation, he shows willingness. I pull out an envelope and slide it towards him.

Before picking it up, he says, 'Do I need to know what's in it?'

'Not yet,' I say. 'But if there ever comes a time when I don't make contact with you, you must open the envelope. The instructions inside will explain what you need to do.'

'Is that it?' he asks.

'There is one more thing,' I say.

I pull out a slip of paper and hand it to him.

When he opens it his eyes narrow, the muscles around them contract, his hand moving the paper back and forth trying his best to get it into focus.

'What is it?' he asks.

'Dates,' I tell him.

'I can see that. What do they mean?'

'The difference between freedom and imprisonment.'

'Okay,' he says.

'You think Campbell would vouch that I was with you guys on these dates, if anyone ever asked?'

Mandrake folds the paper in two and places it inside his jacket pocket along with the envelope.

'I'm sure he would,' he says. 'For some crazy reason, he likes you.'

'And you?'

'Me? I'm just in it for the drinks.'

As we get up Mandrake holds his hand out to me.

'Good luck, kid,' he says.

I reach out, his grip firm, but only in the way I imagine true friendship to feel like. Mandrake once told me many battles can be fought and won if safeguards are put in place. I believe Mandrake builds walls to protect himself, high enough so people can't get to him, and strong enough to withstand the most brutal of attacks. The pugnacious expression, the don't-give-a-shit attitude, they're just bricks in that wall placed there to save him from truly getting hurt. Similarly to how Rebecca spoke of my father, to know Mandrake is to know the true spirit of survival. Maybe a lot has to do with Pam, or the fact I have shown a great deal of trust in him, but today he appears happier, less protective, as if over the last few days he has spent every hour God has granted dismantling that wall brick by brick. I can only assume the mighty Mandrake has finally reached a point in his life where he wishes to feel the grass beneath his feet once more. To dismantle all he has built around him to allow another in.

As for my safeguard: every picture Prudence took, all the dates and times we committed murder, they all lie in the inside pocket of Mandrake's jacket, close to his heart.

Before I leave, I order him a drink.

'You not staying?' he asks once Pam has moved away.

'I have things to do,' I tell him.

'You'll miss Campbell's grand unveiling.'

'I can't stay,' I tell him.

'Probably best, she's so ugly I nearly passed out. It's going to be hard for me to say anything complementary.'

'I'm sure you'll find something,' I tell him.

A man like Mandrake will always find something to say.

CHAPTER 34

The sky burns red and orange, its downy underbelly vanishing behind the horizon ahead of me. In the rear-view mirror, sunlight bouncing off the asphalt burns my eyes leaving me unable to look back from where I came, which is not a bad thing. The grip on the steering wheel is tight, has been for the last twenty miles or more. I'm chasing the shadow of my car down desolate roads that pull me towards her.

What you do today, you do to understand.

I knock back half a can of cola hoping the sugar and caffeine will keep me awake long enough to reach the next town. Old Polaroids taken by Prudence when she was growing up decorate the dashboard, her life laid out. The little things that make the difference. Riding shotgun is a local newspaper open at the obituaries. What I'm looking for are the elderly, people of a certain age. What I'm looking for are clues to where I can find her.

Another hotel.

The man behind the desk has a birthmark on his neck the same shape as an aeroplane window. He takes the picture I have of Prudence, hands shaking slightly, breath smelling like attic boxes. He looks at me and shakes his head. I tell him her name and he shrugs two big fat shoulders. This guy could be the brother of the guy from the last town, the distant cousin of the one before, the uncle of the first.

'She may have given a different name, possibly Felicity.'

He curls out his bottom lip and hands me back the picture. My neck aches, my shoulders too. I ask him how much a room is and he just points to a sign next to the door: £30. I pull out the cash and he counts it in front of a small television he's been watching. The reception is bad so I don't even ask if the room has a television.

The smell inside the hotel room reminds me of the time Verity caught pneumonia and spent two days in a fever. Her skin was wet, pushing out the fever from every pore. Clothes were saturated within seconds, hair lastingly intertwined. Clothes absorb this perfume. You can try, but suffering never leaves the place it has found a home. It's the same with money; it traps the fragrance of the person who owned it before. Sometimes I find myself breathing in the aroma of each note I take delivery of in the hope one holds the sweet smell of Prudence. But none ever do.

I place my overnight bag down and collapse on the bed. Beneath me springs as hard as fists press against my spine, my ribs. The smell of sweat gets worse the nearer I am to the sheets. I fall asleep and awake to a banging close near my head, the soft murmur of ecstasy, of words I remember. I flick on the bedside lamp and look at my watch. Three hours have passed. Next door, the murmurs blossom into screams and drawn-out words of passion.

People only come to these places to have sex or run away.

I reach into my bag and pull out two birthday cards.

The first was hand delivered by Anne Marie. The second came by mail. I open Anne Marie's and it shows a picture of a cartoon boy in a cartoon car driving over cartoon hills. Anne Marie has signed it under the words, Happy Birthday. Part of me feels bad for not telling her about Harry, not that she would show any remorse considering she only spoke with him over the phone. I felt a responsibility to let her know of his death, if only to divest the guilt I've carried since discovering his body two days ago.

The second birthday card is much nicer. It shows a boy sat on a humpback bridge; a homemade rod in his hand hangs down to a tiny stream. It reads: Jack, I hope you have a wonderful birthday. Too many years have slipped by, too many cards unsent. I hope this will be the first of many. Sincerely, Rebecca. X

I place the cards back into my bag and pull out a quart of single malt. My head falls heavy on the pillow. The scent of every other person who has slept here feeds me with thoughts of Prudence and her actions.

Where are you, Prudence?

I am desperate to tell you about something that happened today. I was in a petrol station, filling up my car when I saw a young girl, she must have been no older than six. She was waiting for her mother in the backseat of an expensive

looking car. When she looked at me I almost wept. She was the most beautiful girl I have ever seen. I smiled, to let her know how beautiful she was, but she didn't smile back. She seemed upset. I gave her a little wave with my hand and she blinked slowly with big eyes. Her clothes were pretty, her hair shaped with expensive scissors and a skilled hand. But she looked so sad. Can you believe that? When her mother came out, and they both drove off the forecourt, I followed them. I don't know why. I guess I wanted to make sure the young girl was feeling better.

I travelled three or four miles from the petrol station before the car turned down a road flanked by tall trees and big houses with ornate gates. Some of the houses you could not see from the road because they were set back so far. Large hedges protected most, each trimmed to sharp, clean edges, like the ones found in my father's graveyard. In our father's graveyard. It was a wonderful road. The type of road you dream of living on. I stopped outside their home with its walls painted brilliant white, bright enough to leave you snow-blind. The gates, they opened by a remote switch. I had the perfect chance to get out of my car and approach them. But as I sat there, watching the mother help the young girl down from her seat, I realised there was nothing I could do. To approach them as a stranger, one unshaven with dark rings around his eyes, it would have startled the girl and worried the mother. I would have scared them both. I left shortly after they entered the house and drove back to the main road. I could not understand how such a pretty girl, who would want for nothing, could look so sad.

I took myself to a nearby pub and found solace in a few drinks. You'll be pleased to know the pub rented rooms and I stayed there that night and did not drive. When I fell asleep, I dreamt of that girl. She was calling me from a rapeseed field, her hair backlit by the sun, her face reflecting in shades of yellow. She was smiling, Prudence. She was smiling just for me, and inside the hurting stopped. All at once, I was filled with hope.

You once told me killing was only a matter of perspective. Like a deer struck by a car, what we were doing could be seen as a humane act, not an evil one. Our victims were suffering and desperate to find an end. Many were not in physical agony, but as you say, there is a pain in the heart and mind that is equal and just as debilitating. And so to understand how to live my last days without fear, they offered their necks because life was all too painful for them. But I struggled to turn off emotion so easily. I felt a deep sadness for our victims. I still do. And my weakness is that I care. I care for you and I believe hope is the scaffold that holds us all up, and without it we crumble.

AUTHOR NOTE

The book you have read is not new. It was published in March 2013 by Snubnose Press, a leading independent publisher at the time dealing with hardboiled thrillers, noir and crime. Back then it had a different title too; To Die Upon a Kiss, a line taken from the play Othello just before he commits suicide, something I thought apt considering the methods Jack and Prudence employed to kill their victims. Two months prior to its release, my first novel had come out, The Sound of Loneliness. It is rare for authors to have two books released so close together, especially a fledging one like me. I remember thinking at the time I had arrived. There was a little buzz too building up around the two books, and the first lot of reviews were favourable for both. Fast forward a year and sales had all but dried up for, To Die Upon a Kiss. That's a not a criticism on indie publishers. It's just the way it is sometimes. I was able to request the rights back some time in 2014/5. I didn't know what to do with the book back then. All I knew was that one day I would revisit it. I never expected it'd take another five years for that to happen, but I'm glad it did.

Distance is a blessing. It allows an author to read the book as if for the first time. Five years had gone by and I had written somewhere in the region of five novels and complied another short story collection. To Die Upon a Kiss was alien to me. So when I jumped back into it, I could see all the ambiguity, the imperfections and clumsiness that my fledging hand had rendered to the page. It also had far too much eroticism. Some may think that there can never be too much eroticism, but I have learnt over the years that you can't write something shocking just to provoke a reaction in your reader. Any action has to serve a purpose. So I toned down a lot of the more explicit paragraphs. I also made another significant change. I always liked books with names in the title; The Importance of Being Earnest; The Great Gatsby; A Prayer for Owen Meany. So I wanted to incorporate the protag's name somehow. During the first draft of the novel, I had played around with, The Death and Life of Sadler Truman (Jack's previous incarnation), but it was lengthy and reminded too much of Arthur Miller's, The Death of a Salesman. I tried, Casualties of Fear and Distraction, as well as, Sympathy for the Dead, both of which I felt too wordy and off-putting. By sheer happenstance, I was travelling to work and Blondie came on the radio singing about her heart of glass. As soon as I got home, Sadler Truman became Jack Glass, and the rest, as they say, is history.

The book is now closer to something I envisaged seven years ago when it was first released. There is a lot that pertains to my mindset of that time, of larger questions about life and death, and while they are still relevant, I have found something else more endearing in the prose. It is a story to me about love, and that however fragile life is, we are much more prepared to face our fears when we are consumed with love. I like to think that Jack finally did find Prudence and they settled down before his heart finally gave out. But this is my version of the story and it may differ from yours. Whatever thoughts you have on their fate, I hope this book gladdened your heart and causes you to think twice before allowing a stranger to make you a cup of tea.

Craig Wallwork, October 2020.

ABOUT THE AUTHOR

Craig Wallwork is the three times nominated Pushcart Prize author of the novels, The Sound of Loneliness, Heart of Glass, and the Tom Nolan detective series of books, Bad People and Labyrinth of the Dolls, as well as the short story collections, Quintessence of Dust, and Gory Hole. His work has appeared in many magazines and journals in both the U.K. and U.S. He lives in England with his wife and two children.

If you enjoyed this book, please support the author and leave a review on Amazon and Goodreads. Independent authors do not have the reach of major publishing houses and rely heavily on word of mouth and the kindness of strangers. By passing this book to a friend, or suggesting they buy a copy themselves, or simply mentioning it on social media, really means a lot and helps other readers make an informed choice.

If you would like to receive news and promotions about Craig's books, subscribe to his newsletter and receive a free ebook.

https://landing-page.craigwallwork.com

A New and Exciting Thriller Series is Now Available from Craig Wallwork

BAD PEOPLE (Book 1)
Three missing children. A Writer. A Detective. And a secret cult. But not all is what it seems. A fast paced thriller that will keep you on the edge of your seat.

LABYRINTH OF THE DOLLS (Book 2)
Tom Nolan is back to track down a serial killer who removes the eyes of their victims and dresses them like dolls. But will his past catch up to him before he has time to find them.

Available in both paperback and ebook on Amazon

Printed in Great Britain
by Amazon